High Society Gangster 2

The Caprese Family

Thomas Long

This book is dedicated to my two shining rays of light, Elijah Malachi and Elisha Maliah Long. You two mean the world to me. My love for you is eternal and infinite. I work hard to give you the best of everything this world has to offer. Nothing but greatness awaits you both. I'm proud to be your Dad!

------T. Long

Chapter 1

The uneasy tension in the room couldn't have been thicker. Geno and Jericho stood face to face in the restroom, with their eyes locked in on one another in a stare down for the Ages. Neither one of them refused to budge an inch. It would go against their pedigree to do so. A true gangster never cowered while in the line of fire, but instead became bolder in his disposition even if he was at a disadvantage. Jericho clearly had the upper hand because he drew his weapon first, but Geno stood firm and held his ground like the tried and true thug he was. Even though he was a shirt and tie business man today, he still possessed the aggressive inner spirit from his younger days when he wasn't afraid to throw hands or use his gun if necessary to resolve a confrontation. Jericho and Geno were two battle tested gladiators from the streets trained not to fear death. However, they both were also smart enough to acknowledge the reality of death and how the Grim Reaper could pay a visit for that final curtain call at any moment. Neither one of them was in a rush to meet such a fate, but accepted it as a part of the lifestyle they chose to live.

As he stared at Jericho, Geno noticed he had many of their biological father's physical features. Jericho inherited his menacing eyes and had the same distinguished dimple in his right cheek. His now deceased brother, Silvio, shared these same physical attributes with Leonardo as well. Geno and Jericho were around the same height and build with the same broad shoulders. Outside of his melanin rich skin tone, Jericho had all of the genetic makeup of a Caprese man.

A part of Geno was curious about Jericho and Shavon and wanted to get to know them. After he read, in detail, the file Lucci had compiled on them, he was enraged they were forced to live in poverty with no financial help at all from Leonardo. He couldn't imagine growing up without a mother and father in his life. He hated Leonardo almost as much as Jericho did for not stepping up to the plate like a man should do to be the best father he could be to his children. Nothing on this Earth could stop him from being involved with raising Gianna and Stefan. His love for them even surpassed the love he had for his soul mate, Carina. They were his legacy. They were the heirs to the massive empire he was in the process of building. All of his hard work was to ensure they would have a future free of financial struggle and hardship. Leonardo's lame excuse about Jericho's mother not allowing him to be a part of their lives was unacceptable to Geno. Leonardo might have been a hard core gangster in the streets, but to Geno he was a coward as a man and father. That carried far more weight as a testament to his true character as far as Geno was concerned. Leonardo's failure as a father was the reason he felt empathy for Jericho even though he currently stood before him with a gun pointed in his direction.

"So, you're the notorious Jericho Jones, huh? I guess I'm lucky to be one of the few people to have ever been able to actually see you in the flesh. I would say it's nice to meet you, but it's kind of hard for me to do considering the fact you have a gun pointed at me," Geno uttered in an attempt to lighten the mood in the room. Jericho failed to see the humor in his statement. His stoic demeanor suggested he was all about business.

"It's good to know that my reputation precedes me. I guess that means I'm pretty good at what I do," he spit back with the cold and calm demeanor of a ruthless assassin well versed in the administration of death.

Jericho was proud of the fact he was able to keep his identity a secret from most of his clients. His anonymity was maintained by calculated design. If none of his clients were able to describe how he looked, they would never be able to testify against him in court if by some unforeseen twist of fate he happened to botch a job and wound up getting arrested. Nearly all of his clients contacted him through Gutta first and were thoroughly vetted before he accepted a job. He was Gutta's secret weapon. He commanded a high price for his services because he delivered as promised every time. The only time he made an exception and met with a client face to face was when the payment for a job was in the six figure range and the client made it a mandatory condition before any money was exchanged. Even in those rare instances, he arranged the meetings in the most remote of locations as possible.

As Jericho stared at Geno, he held his pistol with a steady grip. It was pointed center mass at Geno's chest. All it took was just one swift movement of his trigger finger to end Geno's life. Jericho loved the power associated with having another's man fate in his hands. He never understood why he got such an adrenaline rush from being able to kill a man with either his bare hands or his choice of weapons, but he accepted it as a part of who he was. He was good at what he did and took pride in his work just as any man who had perfected his craft would. Just like Michael Jordan was cocky about what he could do on the basketball court, Jericho approached his job in the same manner. He knew there was no man alive more skilled than him at delivering death in a multitude of ways.

To his advantage, Geno thrived off of his own knack to be able to improvise and think quickly on his feet to get himself out of hostile situations in both the streets and the business world. He needed every bit of his superior skill set to get him out of his current predicament. His continued existence on this Earth depended on his ability to do so. He studied Jericho's demeanor in hopes he might detect a hint of fear or weakness in him, but there was none to be found. There were no chinks in his armor visible for him to exploit. He didn't display any outward signs of self-doubt as to whether or not he would pull the trigger and kill Geno if he chose to do so. Jericho was the real deal.

Geno had been in the presence of many ruthless killers in his lifetime and Jericho possessed the same black hearted spirit inside of him that they did. Jericho was rock solid with the heart of lion. He was the kind of soldier Geno would love to recruit to be a part of his family because die hard soldiers were hard to find in this current day and time. Most of the young upstarts in the streets today were nothing more than trigger happy young fools eager to build a reputation as opposed to the well trained assassins he utilized along the way in his rise to the top of the food chain in the underworld. Jericho was definitely a throwback to the golden era of gangsters.

The look in Jericho's eyes was one of pure evil intent. He was clearly an angry young man and rightfully so given his tumultuous upbringing. He had the demeanor of a man with a chip on his shoulder which served as the driving force behind his every action. Men like Jericho didn't need an external catalyst to be set in motion to cause mass destruction. Violence just came natural for him. Every death he caused was all about business and nothing more. He never questioned his clients' motives for seeking to have his victims killed because it didn't matter. As long as his clients paid his agreed upon price for his services rendered, he made sure the contract was fulfilled flawlessly. This scenario was different because he wasn't paid to kill Geno. He had an emotional connection to the situation at hand. If he decided to kill Geno, it would be for personal satisfaction.

In spite of his clear advantage, for some strange reason, Jericho was in no rush to end Geno's life. He felt mixed emotions now that he finally had a chance to meet him face to face. On one hand, his mind raged with feelings of sheer jealousy and envy at the fact he had to grow up fatherless in the ghetto while Leonardo played the role of a father to Geno and his other siblings. He gave them the love, wisdom, and attention Jericho so desperately sought after as a child. He wanted Geno to feel some of the emotional pain and anguish him and Shavon felt being fatherless. Because of Leonardo's absence, Jericho was forced to grow up fast to survive in the rough streets of Baltimore City. The bumps and bruises he endured along the way lingered in his mind. Even though he knew Geno wasn't responsible for the hand he was dealt, he felt a desire to take out all of the animosity he felt for Leonardo on him. He knew how much Geno meant to Leonardo and if he were to kill him, it would bring him a slight level of joy to see Leonardo suffer emotionally the same way he did when his mother died in that horrific fire many years ago.

On the other hand, he was curious to know more about Geno because even though he loved Shavon with all of his heart, he always wanted a big brother. He was no different from any other young Black male who grew up in the inner city in a fatherless home. He never had a positive male role model to emulate growing up. The only male he connected with was his mentor, Gutta, who taught him all he knew about the street life and the murder game. When he was younger, he dreamed his father would come along one day and whisk him, his mother, and Shavon away from their life of poverty to live in a big house with a white picket fence. That day never came. As a result, he was forced to take on the role of the man of the house when he was just a boy ill equipped to do so.

Jericho believed that if he had a positive father figure in his life growing up, his life would be totally different. He reasoned that maybe he wouldn't be as cold hearted as he turned out to be. Left to his own devices, his life had become a vicious cycle of nothing but death and drama. He wanted out of the dangerous lifestyle he lived, but didn't know how to escape. He felt trapped with no way out. Even though he considered himself the best at what he did, he knew his lucky run of never serving time or having to face retaliation for his violent actions wouldn't last forever.

Jericho had nightmares about his life ending in a hail of gunfire or him serving a life sentence once karma caught up with him. As he glanced at Geno, he wondered if he could be that big brother or male voice of reason and support he sought for so many years to lead him in another direction with a more positive ending. If he killed him, he would never find out. He might also miss out on a golden opportunity to develop a bond with his biological brother. He had to make a choice to decide which voice in his head to follow very quickly.

"You've got me dead to right. If you're going to kill me, then let's get it over with, Jericho. Let's not waste any more time. However, if you're not going to kill me, then lower that gun and let's talk like gentleman. I'm sure we can work something out between us. You know I'ma wealthy man and I can make things happen in this town. I believe you love money just as much as I do. I can get you plenty of it to spend however you want," Geno offered in an attempt to save his life.

"You think this is about money? You can keep your money. I've got more than enough of my own.

You saw my resume. I think it gave you a clear picture I'm the best at what I do and I've been paid top dollar for my services. Money is not an issue for me," Jericho stated resolutely with his weapon still pointed at Geno.

"I can respect that and I hear where you're coming from, Jericho. I apologize if I offended you. That was not my intention at all. I'm sure you have a lot of questions running through your head right now about me and our father. Let me just say, until recently, I never knew you existed. Our father kept you and Shavon as his little secret all of these years. I believe the only reason he told me now is because he's dying from cancer and he's trying make peace with God for his past sins. When I found out about you, I felt betrayed. I haven't spoken to him since. I couldn't believe he could do such a wicked thing to deny his own kin. That's not the man I know. The Leonardo Caprese who raised me was involved in my life every step of the way. I don't know what went wrong with him when it came to the two of you. My heart goes out to you and Shavon. I mean that sincerely. I can't even begin to imagine how you must feel right now. All I can say is had I known about you years ago, things would have been different for both of us. I can't turn back the hands of time. What's done is done. Like it or not, you're flesh of my flesh and we share a similar bloodline. Why don't you put that gun down and let's work this thing out?" Geno suggested. Judging by the now befuddled look on his face, Geno's words struck a chord with Jericho.

"I haven't had a family all of these years and I don't need one now! I wanted to look you in your eyes to see for myself what was so special about you that made him be a father to you and not me. Now, that I met you, I'm not impressed at all. You're no better than me. I want to make you suffer," Jericho ranted in a blind fury.

He was out of character because it was unlike him to let any form of emotion show publicly, but he couldn't contain himself. For so many years these feelings had been bottled up inside and now they just flowed out like a tidal wave. He felt this same intense rush of emotions right before he killed Roger Dandy, the slumlord responsible for his mother's death. Watching him and his brother, Jim, suffer before they met their demise gave him some sense of relief, but it didn't repair the emotional scars he had from his mother's death. Nothing could fill that void for him. He began to wonder if killing Geno would take away the pain and anger he held inside against Leonardo for all of these years.

Jericho took a step back and wrapped his hand tightly around his gun like he was about to fire, but couldn't bring himself to squeeze the trigger. He had never frozen up when it was kill time in his life, but he had also never killed a blood relative before. Even though he didn't know him, Geno was his blood. This was a mitigating factor he couldn't ignore. It was as though there was a divine force intervening which caused his hesitation. In observing him, Jericho too noticed the resemblance he and Geno shared to one another. He couldn't deny they were kin. Nonetheless, his heart was still filled with rage and envy. His rational mind knew Geno was not to blame for them not having a relationship. That blame lied squarely on Leonardo's shoulders. As he waged a battle with the voices in his head, Geno took his moment of reprieve as an opportunity to try and flip the script on Jericho.

"I understand how you feel, Jericho, but let's not do something foolish here. I'm sure you know about my reputation as well. You look like the kind of man that does his research before he acts. I think you should know if I don't get back to my family soon, my men, who are right outside of the bathroom door, will come looking for me shortly. This could get ugly for both of us," Geno attempted to reason with him.

Jericho seemed unfazed by the thought of being confronted by Geno's goons. That was because he was confident in his ability to kill them both without suffering the slightest injury to himself. He was a master of the art of delivering either a slow, painful death sentence or one that was quick and painless. He had no reason to feel any fear. He was built for situations like this one. Truth be told,

Geno's goons should be the ones in fear of what he could do to them. He had already sized up Geno's security detail and surmised they were no match for him. He could put a bullet between the eyes of both of Geno's goons way before they would have a chance to get to their weapons. Armed with this information, Jericho's cocky swagger was on full display.

"Trust me, Geno; your men are no threat to me. I could've killed them already if I wanted to with no problem whatsoever. I'ma beast of a whole different kind of nature than those hired hands you have out there. They protect you for the money, but I kill for pleasure. It gives me a thrill to see a man take his last breath and to know I'm the one that took his life. The concept of death doesn't bother me at all. I died inside a long time ago," Jericho rebutted.

"Let's just get this over with, Jericho. I'm not going to beg for my life. I'm too much of a stand up guy to go out groveling on my knees like a spineless coward. There's no need to waste any more time. I'm ready to meet my maker. I know Hell has a place waiting for me. Let's do this," Geno shot back defiantly in an attempt to call Jericho's bluff.

"Relax, Geno, I think I'll let you live for now. Besides, you were right about us having some business to discuss," Jericho stated. He lowered his gun down by his side. He had a wicked smile on his face. He chuckled devilishly. It sounded even more sinister due to the echo effect caused by the bathroom's vaulted ceilings.

"Well, if money doesn't interest you, then tell me what you want so we can both walk out of this situation satisfied. However, before we get to the business at hand, I want to know how you found me here?" Geno asked curiously. If he made it out of this situation alive, his hired guns would surely be dealt with for their incompetence. He felt relieved his life was being spared. For all of his bravado, he wasn't ready to die just yet. He had many more things to accomplish.

"I'm a very resourceful person, but I think you know that already. I got the message from your guy, John Lucci, through a mutual associate that you were looking for me. I've been following you for a minute, clocking your every movement. I figured this very public place was the best venue for me to introduce myself to you. You have a very beautiful family," Jericho replied.

"Thank you for the compliment. My family is everything to me. Just like you, I will kill for what I love. Well, let's cut to the chase, Jericho. Let's stop the mind games. Tell me what you want," Geno demanded. He was clearly getting more agitated by the minute. He took Jericho's mentioning his family as a veiled threat. If Jericho even dreamed about harming one hair on the heads of either his children or his wife, Geno would inflict just as much pain and suffering upon him and the ones he loved. He could be just as evil and heartless as Jericho if provoked.

"I hear you're the best attorney money can buy in Baltimore. I understand you're well connected everywhere and can make things happen. Is that true?" Jericho asked.

"Yes, it is the truth. If you find a better lawyer than me in this State, I'll pay you six figures in cash money. I'm not bragging, but I'm just stating the truth," Geno stated boldly. He, just like Jericho, had an unwavering level of confidence in his abilities when it came to his area of expertise.

"Well, then I guess you're the man for the job. My sister, I mean *our* sister, Shavon, was raped by her boyfriend. She was totally traumatized by what happened, but that's not all. When my girlfriend, Nina, found out about what happened, she went over to his house and killed him in retaliation. She emptied a whole clip into him like it was nothing. The dude's name was Marcus Harrison. You may have seen the story mentioned on the news a while back. When I found out about what happened, I was on my way to kill Marcus myself, but Nina beat me to the punch. That's how I got pulled into this situation. The police have a witness who saw us leave Marcus' house and can identify us. He gave the cops a description of the three of us. They have warrants out for our arrest. With all of the drug related murders that take place in the city every day, I know they're not spending a lot of time looking for us, but I would rather be safe than sorry. We don't plan to live the rest of our lives on the run. I've got Nina and Shavon stashed away safely for now. They're somewhere the cops won't even think to look for them. I need you to work your magic and make this whole thing go away so we can get back to our regular lives. I need you to name your price and I'll pay it no matter how much it is," Jericho replied rather straightforward and honestly. It was a tall order to ask this of Geno, but from the information he had gathered about him and the far reach of his power and influence, it wasn't something he couldn't make happen.

"I'm so sorry to hear about what happened to Shavon. Any bastard who has to rape a woman should be put inside of a cage with a dozen pit bulls. I would pay to see them tear the flesh from his bones until he bled to death. A rapist is the lowest form of scum on the Earth to me. If I can do this for you, what will I get in return besides money?" Geno asked. He was genuinely upset to hear about the rape. The fact she was his half-sister made it hit home even more. His mother always taught him it was a man's job to respect and protect a woman. She told him only a coward put his hands on a woman. She instilled this ideology into him from the time he was a child and it became a part of his character to always hold a lady in the highest regard.

"You'll get to live and won't have to worry about having me as an enemy. I think that's a fair trade off," Jericho replied coldly.

He was intrigued by Geno's idea of using pit bulls to kill a rapist. He like the idea so much he considered trying it in the very near future. For now, he needed to stay focused on the task at hand. He knew he just made a bold statement to Baltimore's biggest gangster, but he didn't care. He had already devised a strategy to deal with Geno if he didn't agree to help him. He didn't plan to shoot him. Using a gun was Jericho's least favorite weapon of choice. He liked to get creative when he came up with a plan to kill somebody. He had a syringe filled with a lethal concoction of cyanide in his pocket ready to inject into Geno's neck. It would kill him in a matter of minutes if he didn't honor his request.

"Jericho, you have yourself a deal. I can make this case go away. I want to help Shavon get all the help she needs as well. No woman should have to endure being violated by a man. Even though I don't know her, she is still my sister as well. You can keep your money. If I do this for you, just know that I'm going to want something from you in return. However, we can discuss that at a later date," Geno stated.

"If you do this for me, I will owe you and I always pay my debts. Like you, I'ma standup guy and my word is my bond. A fair exchange is never a robbery in my book. You deliver for me and I'll do the same in return. Oh, and on another note, you might want to beef up security. Their movements are too predictable. I could've killed you on numerous occasions and got away with ease," Jericho advised him.

"Your words are duly noted. We have ourselves a deal," Geno replied.

Jericho shook Geno's hand to solidify their agreement. He handed him a business card that had a cell phone number hand written on the back of it for him to use to contact him once the job was complete. Shortly thereafter, Jericho made his way to the door to exit the restroom. When he walked out of the bathroom, he briskly strolled right past Geno's two goons, who were positioned on both sides of the door. They had no clue Geno could've died on their watch. In their defense, they did a sweep of the bathroom before Geno entered, but they didn't see Jericho because he stood on top of a toilet seat inside of one of the stalls. Jericho disappeared in the crowd of people exiting the fashion show just as quickly as he had appeared out of nowhere.

Geno left out of the restroom a few minutes after Jericho to rejoin his family. He acted as though everything was fine and he didn't just face a near death experience. He was mad Jericho was able to track him down so easily because his enemies could possibly do the same. He would definitely have to take heed to Jericho's advice and implement new security measures. Nonetheless, he finally had a chance to meet his half brother, albeit not under the most cordial circumstances. There was no bloodshed and a pact was made between the two Caprese men which he planned to honor. Once he made this case disappear, he wanted to make the time to get to know Jericho and Shavon if they were amenable to the idea. After all, they were his family regardless of how that came to pass. The whole trip home, Geno was silent as he processed what just went down.

Chapter 2

Jericho felt a sense of victory and relief after his meeting with Geno. He thought he had Geno right where he wanted him to make him do what he needed him to do. He was pretty good at reading people and could sense Geno was a man of his word. While Geno did whatever he needed to do, he would just have to be patient and wait. He hated asking for help from anyone because he felt powerless and he associated that with weakness. To be at another man's mercy went against his nature. However, in this instance, he had no choice but to humble himself. Geno was his best option to make this whole matter go away.

As he drove back to the safe house where he had Nina and Shavon stashed away, he was careful not to go over the speed limit or run any stop lights because he didn't want to draw attention to himself from the police. His picture, along with ones of Shavon and Nina, were blasted all over the news as persons of interest in the case when the police discovered Marcus' body. That fact made him even more mindful he needed to move about town cautiously.

Whenever he went out in the public, he made sure he altered his appearance so as to not look anything like the mug shot photo of him shown on the news. The photo of him was taken from the one time he was arrested for allegedly committing an armed robbery when he was eighteen years old. The charges in that case were dropped due to a lack of evidence and the robbery victim being afraid to testify. All Jericho needed was to be pulled over by some overeager cop on a humble for a traffic violation to wind up being carted off to jail after the cop ran his driver's license and saw he had an open warrant out for his arrest. If that were to happen, Jericho didn't intend to be carted off to jail peacefully. He had every intention of holding court in the streets and taking out as many police officers as he could. He had no reservation about killing a police officer if he stood in the way of his own freedom. He hated law enforcement officers, in particular Baltimore City cops, with a passion because of their long documented history of brutality against young Black men.

With all of the murders he actually committed which the police had no way to tie to him, he couldn't believe he was now on their radar for a body that wasn't even his to claim. He was mad at himself for getting caught slipping. He let his emotions, being upset about Shavon being raped, get the best of him. They clouded his judgment when he made the decision to go to Marcus' house and kill him for what he did to his sister. He yearned to get back to living the anonymous existence he enjoyed for so many years.

His journey through the mean streets of Baltimore gave him a chance to get a good glance at the impoverished conditions which inner city residents lived under on a daily basis. The sight of dope fiends, alcoholics, and crack addicts on a hunt for their next fix was an all too familiar sight for him. They all reminded him of the characters who littered the streets of his East Baltimore neighborhood when he lived with his grandparents as a teenager. While these individuals weren't the same people from his neighborhood, their story was the same. He saw the suffering on their faces as they traveled recklessly in the night in a city where death lurked around every corner. They all were on a mission to escape the harsh reality of their very existence.

Jericho was haunted by the images of herds of young Black men who were around his age or younger posted up on virtually every ghetto corner he passed by engaged in some form of criminal behavior just to survive. They were trapped in a hopeless reality of selling and using drugs which usually ended up with them being carted off back and forth to the penitentiary for years at a time or shot dead on the street. Jericho felt sorry for them. He came from the same hopeless place they did, but he was thankful their current reality wasn't his reality.

Jericho felt like he beat the odds of what was expected of a young Black man from the ghetto because he hadn't experienced the harshness of prison life thus far. Yet, here he stood, as a fugitive on the run, just like them, for a crime he didn't commit. It seemed unjust to be in such a situation, but he failed to factor in the reality of karma's strange way of rearing its head in the most unsuspecting moments. He might not have killed Marcus, but he damn sure had more than enough dead bodies to answer for on Judgment Day.

When he reached the safe house, Jericho turned off the headlights and slowly pulled the car into the garage. The house was located on a three acre farm property off of exit 24 on Interstate 83 North in a remote section of Baltimore County. It was a property Gutta wisely purchased years ago to be used only in situations such as this one. The house was small in size, approximately fifteen hundred square feet in total, but it contained everything they needed to survive. Gutta bought it for cash from the previous owner under an alias name so it couldn't be tied to him in any way. If he were ever in a situation where he was on the run from the police and needed to lay low for a while before he left town, the farm was the perfect place to hide out. His closest neighbor was about a mile up the road. No one would think to look for him in such a clandestine place. When Jericho called him in a panic the night Marcus was killed in need of a place to stash Nina and Shavon, Gutta let him use the house without hesitation because he and Jericho were like family. While Jericho did what he had to do to take care of the situation, Gutta agreed to stay at the house with Nina and Shavon to ensure their safety.

As Jericho walked through the small shack, he heard the television playing in the living room area. He expected to see Gutta situated on the couch with the remote control in his hand, but when he reached the room, there was no one there. He looked in the kitchen and saw it was empty as well. Just as he was about to turn around and walk toward the bathroom, he was greeted by the barrel of a gun up against his temple. He froze in his tracks. Somebody had the drop on him. He was in no position to get to the gun he had stashed in his dip. He put his hands up on his head as a sign of his surrender. He always knew his life would end in a blaze of gunfire he never saw coming. He closed his eyes and readied himself for the loud banging sound the gun would make once its owner squeezed the trigger.

"You see how I just caught you off guard, young blood? I could have easily been a cop or one of your many enemies. Your reaction time is off. You're slipping, Jericho. I taught you to be sharp and on point at all times," Gutta stated before he lowered his weapon.

"Stop playing around, Gutta, I wasn't scared. I knew it was you," Jericho spat back in an attempt to save face. Jericho knew Gutta spoke the truth. He wasn't on his A game at the moment, but was relieved it was his trusted companion and not the police or one of his enemies because he would definitely be a dead man right now. He was glad to be granted a reprieve from death once again. They both walked into the living to continue their conversation.

"You didn't know a damn thing, Jericho. I could've splattered your brains on the wall and you would've never seen it coming. Never mind that, man, tell me how the meeting went," Gutta inquired.

"Everything went just like I planned for things to go. Geno and I had a nice long talk. He's going to play ball because he knows it's in his best interest to do so," Jericho replied.

"You took one hell of a chance messing with that cat. He's a heavy hitter in the streets. I still can't believe he's your half brother," Gutta stated.

"Yeah, well he never met a killer like me. I caught him totally by surprise," Jericho bragged.

"How did it feel being face to face with him for the first time?" Gutta asked.

"Let's just say we had a long talk about our father and I learned a few interesting things tonight I plan to follow up on. He appears to be a stand up guy and about his word. That's enough about Geno. Where are my girls at?" Jericho responded while changing the subject.

"That's good news, Jericho. I'm glad you were able to connect with him, but I still say you need to be careful. He's a dangerous and manipulative man. I've got your back if you need me. As for Nina and Shavon, they're in the bedroom. Shavon still won't eat a thing. Nina is doing the best she can with her, Jericho, but she's in bad shape. She needs to see a head doctor. Her mind is all messed up right now."

"She's going to be okay. She just needs more time. Once Geno takes care of this business for us, I'll get her all of the help she needs."

Gutta just shook his head as Jericho walked past him. He knew Jericho was in denial about the reality of Shavon's state of mind. She was still in a state of shock as a result of the rape. She appeared to be suffering from post traumatic stress disorder. As a veteran of the Vietnam War, Gutta had firsthand knowledge of the signs and symptoms of

PTSD. He knew Shavon needed professional help from a psychiatrist if she had any chance at becoming a fully functional human being of sound mind again. However, the longer she went without psychotherapy, the more of an uphill road she had to climb to get back to normal, if that was at all possible.

When Jericho walked into the master bedroom, he saw Nina rocking back and forth as she held Shavon in her arms. Tears streamed down Shavon's face. She mumbled a series of words incoherently. Nina did her best to keep her calm and to comfort her. Jericho felt a sharp pain in his chest as he observed Shavon in such a fragile state. He was used to seeing her as the lively college student who was on course to become an attorney. Her warm, jovial spirit was replaced by the image of a broken woman who was mentally and emotionally unstable. She had lost a good amount of weight, her hair was unkempt, and she looked nothing like his beautiful, innocent little sister. She was a shell of her former self. As he stared at her, he thought about all of the years he took care of her and shielded her from harm. He was mad at himself for not being there to protect her from a monster like Marcus. He blamed himself for her current condition. When Shavon looked up and saw him, her eyes lit up. Even in her delusional state of mind she recognized her big brother.

"Jericho, please save me from these demons in here! They're everywhere! The monsters are coming to get me! They are coming for me!" Shavon rambled on. She was clearly detached from reality and hallucinating. She rarely slept anymore. Whenever she did, it would be for short periods of time before she awoke as a result of having the same recurring dream about the night Marcus stole her innocence from her. Nina moved to the side when Jericho sat down on the bed so he could hold Shavon in his arms. She got up and walked out of the room for a moment because she had to use the bathroom.

"No one is coming for you, Shavon. You're safe. Big brother is here. I'll protect you," Jericho uttered in an effort to comfort her. Her tears fell on his broad shoulders as he held her in his arms. He wanted to kill somebody to release his frustration from having to see Shavon in such a fragile state.

"I just talked to Mommy. She told me to tell you not to worry yourself so much because everything is going to be alright. She said she's going to come live with us and we're going to be a family just like we were when we were kids," Shavon rambled on hysterically. Her mind took her back to a time in her childhood when she felt safe and secure.

"That's right, baby sis, we're all going to be together again one day as a family. However, right now I need you to get some rest and let us take care of you," Jericho replied. He too wished he could talk to his mother at least one more time because he never stopped missing her since the day she died.

"She's like this all day. She won't eat much at all. I got her to eat a little bit of soup earlier, but then she just threw it back up. You can see how much weight she has lost, Jericho. We need to do something else to help her. I don't know what else to do. She needs to see a doctor badly. I'm going to turn myself in to the police and tell them everything. I'm going to tell them that I'm the one that killed Marcus because it's the truth. You two shouldn't have to suffer because of what I did," Nina attempted to reason with him when she returned to the room.

"You need to stop talking crazy, Nina. You are not turning yourself into the police. Why would you do something so foolish? Marcus deserved to die after what he did. You know it's true. Anyway, this will all be over with soon. I'm working on fixing this whole situation for us. We just have to be patient for a minute. Don't worry, Shavon, your big brother is going to take care of everything. Nina, I've got the situation under control. You just have to trust me," he stated confidently.

"Okay, baby, if you say so. I never question your judgment. We're a family and we're in this together until the end," Nina stated.

Jericho held Shavon in his arms tightly to console her as best he could. Nina sat back down on

the bed on the other side of Shavon and wrapped
her arms around her as well. Their warm embrace
seemed to temporarily give Shavon a sense of
comfort as she drifted off to sleep. They were three
young Black children who grew up victimized by
the harsh realities of urban ghetto life. With no
righteous guidance from a positive adult figure in
their lives growing up, they were forced to fend for
themselves the best way they knew how. Fate made
them become a family. They needed each other now
more than ever to make it through their current
predicament.

Chapter 3

Geno's mind was at ease even though he had what seemed to be a trying task in front of him. He had no doubt in his ability to make good on his promise to have Jericho, Shavon, and Nina exonerated of all charges. It took him a minute to come up with the ideal plan, but when he did, he just needed all of the pieces to fall into place perfectly for it to work. What he had in mind was unethical and illegal and could cost him his law license as well as his freedom if he slipped up in any way. However, it wasn't like it was something new for him to straddle the legal fence to get something done. Geno did whatever was necessary to accomplish his goals. All of the players involved in his plan needed to do exactly as instructed so nothing could be traced back to him.

Thanks to the hard work of John Lucci, he had a black book full of useful information at his disposal to use as leverage to get all of the necessary individuals to play ball with him if it were necessary to go that route. Just the threat of public exposure of their dirty deeds done behind closed doors was enough to get them to do his bidding whenever he needed something from one of them. Geno was not above resorting to such underhanded tactics to get the job done. Any wreckage caused along the way was just collateral damage. His only concern was to achieve the desired end result.

Geno sat behind the desk in his office at Maggie's and puffed on a fresh Cuban cigar. In front of him on his desk was a copy of the Marcus Harrison case file for him to review. He got the file from a clerk in the police department who was known to be on the take for years. He wanted to be fully aware of what evidence the police actually had to get a clear picture of what he was up against. The autopsy results indicated the cause of death was from multiple gunshot wounds. Marcus' damaged front door indicated there was a forced entry by someone and that robbery couldn't be ruled out as a motive. However, the police were going off of the theory this case was a crime of passion whereby Marcus was killed either intentionally or accidentally by a female associate. This theory was based on the fact that the witness who came forward claimed to have overheard a verbal confrontation take place between Marcus and a female just a few minutes before he heard the fatal gunshots ring out. The gunshots were followed up shortly thereafter by Jericho coming along and kicking the door off of the hinges when he entered the house.

The eyewitness gave a detailed physical description of Jericho, Nina, and Shavon to the police. The name of the eyewitness was not mentioned in the file, but that was a minor detail for Geno because he had the means to get the person's information. To know the witness' identity was critical to him being able to put his plan into motion. The police were building their case around this person's testimony. However, if there was no witness to testify, then there would be no case. Consequently, the State would have no choice but to drop the charges. He had a meeting scheduled tonight with a person who could get him just what he needed to make this entire case disappear before it got a chance to even get to court.

While he waited for his guest to arrive, Geno sipped on a glass of cognac with his feet up on his desk and his chair leaned all the way back in a reclining position. He had a full day in court earlier and was exhausted, but this piece of business needed to be handled expeditiously. He stared up at the ceiling and, in a moment of reflection, thought about his life and all of the hard work he put in and the sacrifices he made to be in the powerful position he currently held being at the helm of the Caprese Foundation. He thought about all of the individuals he blackmailed, all of the streets wars he engaged in, and all of the lives lost along his journey to the top of his empire. He saw it all as necessary evils he had to endure to achieve the greater good which was his success. He regretted having to kill his own brother, but he knew he had no choice but to do so. Silvio's envy and jealousy of Geno would have wound up costing him his life if he didn't strike first. When he told Cesare he had Silvio killed, initially Cesare was upset. However, after he gave him a detailed explanation, he accepted it as a realistic consequence of the life they led.

In the streets, a family member was the worst kind of enemy to have because of the emotional ties involved. A street soldier had to have a special genetic makeup to be able to kill his own flesh and blood without hesitation if he wanted to remain a major player in the underworld. Geno had the boldness and audacity to make that hard decision because it was necessary to fortify his position of power.

After the brutal manner in which he dismantled Nesta and his crew and walked away virtually unscathed, Geno's actions further fortified his already solid street credibility. It was clear to the entire Baltimore underworld that Geno Caprese was untouchable and the most powerful man in the city. He had the streets in fear of his wrath. Even his business partners, the Jackson brothers, who were deadly in their own right, knew not to cross him.

"Geno, the man you were waiting for is here now. Should I send him back?" his burly bodyguard, Milo, asked after he knocked first and was given permission by Geno to enter.

"Yes, you can bring him back," Geno replied. He put his cigar out and sat up in his chair. He readied himself to put forth his most professional face to conduct the business at hand. Within a few minutes, his guest was ushered into his office. The man was an average height with a slender build. His partially gray hair suggested he was somewhere in his mid-forties or early fifties. He was dressed in a sharp navy blue suit and had a tan colored fedora hat in his hand. He appeared to be uneasy and nervous to be in Geno's presence. Geno tended to have that effect on people because of his larger than life personality. Nonetheless, he sat down in the seat on the other side of Geno's desk so they could have a conversation.

"Police Commissioner Leftwich, my friend, I haven't seen you in a while. I hope all is well with Samantha and the kids," he uttered.

"My family is fine, Geno. Thanks for asking. Now tell me what you want so we can make this short, simple, and sweet. I have more important business to tend to than to be in the presence of a no good criminal bastard like you," Leftwich uttered.

In spite of the cordial manner in which Geno greeted him, he couldn't stand the sight of Geno Caprese. He held the same level of disdain for him that God had for the Devil. If he had his way, Geno would be a dead man. He seethed with anger at the sarcastic manner in which Geno pretended to care about his family because he knew Geno didn't give a damn about them. Herman would love to pull out his Baltimore City issued, Glock 22 .40 caliber pistol and empty the entire clip into Geno to end his life. However, Geno had dirt on him which could put him behind bars if it were to be placed in the hands of the appropriate parties so it was in his best interest that Geno remained alive.

Leftwich was a closet homosexual and child molester who loved to have sex with underage Black boys even though he was married with children of his own. Geno had a folder full of nude pictures and text and chat room messages that Leftwich had exchanged with various teenage boys at his disposal that he used to blackmail him on numerous occasions to get Leftwich to use his position as the top cop in the City for whatever purpose he deemed necessary. Geno had him by the balls and Herman despised him because of that fact. However, he had no one to blame for his predicament but himself. He chose to be a slimy pervert who preyed on children. Geno simply exploited his knowledge of his illicit behavior to get what he needed from him.

"There is no need to be hostile, Herman. There's no need for the name calling either. Let's try and be civil here. Besides, if I'm allegedly a criminal because of my actions, then we both have that in common, would you not agree? Now, with that out of the way, let me pour you a drink," Geno offered him calmly while he poured himself another glass of cognac. He noticed a drastic shift in Herman's demeanor instantly. He went from an aggressive disposition to one of a man who just had a taste of humble pie.

"What the hell, you might as well pour me a drink. I'm going to need one because I know you want something from me that's going to leave my head spinning," Herman replied.

Geno got up from behind his desk to retrieve another glass from his mini-bar and poured him a drink. Herman took the drink straight to the head. Geno shook his head at the way he gulped down the alcohol. Herman clearly had no class because a man who appreciated a good stiff drink sipped it slowly to savor the flavor as opposed to taking it straight to the head like a homeless wino. Geno returned to his seat and reclined back while he put his feet up on the desk. He sat with his arms folded and a big smile on his face. He flicked the ashes from his cigar into the ashtray and exhaled a large cloud of smoke into the air.

"It's nothing too serious, Herman, my man. It's something I know you can handle. I just need a little information is all," Geno said rather calmly.

"Your definition of a little information is something that can change the landscape of the power structure in the City. You know I know how you operate, Geno. Nothing you do is harmless and innocuous. Now, with that being said, what do you need from me?" Herman inquired.

"Well, there's an open murder case involving a man named Marcus Harrison. I need the name of the witness by the end of the week. I need this case to go away," Geno requested forcefully.

"You want me to give you the name of a police witness so you can kill him or her? I can't do that Geno. Asking me to make a drug case go away or to cut somebody loose on a domestic violence charge is one thing, but you're talking about something else here. Giving you the name of an informant is like me sanctioning murder because I know what you plan to do to the person. I won't do it, Geno," Herman stated in an attempt to stand his ground. This request was clearly a step up from others Geno had made in the past. As the top cop in Baltimore City, he would have hell to pay if it were ever discovered he leaked confidential police information on an open murder case.

"Perhaps I didn't make myself clear enough, Herman. This wasn't a request. It's a demand. You will do what I ask you to do when I tell you to do it with no questions asked. I own you. You work for me. If you don't agree, I'll be more than happy to show my little folder full of dirty pictures of you having sex with those young boys to the wonderful mayor of Baltimore City. I'm sure he would find this information interesting to say the least," Geno threatened. It was obvious that Herman was shaken up by the way he moved about nervously in his seat.

"Geno, please don't ask me to do this. I'm begging you. If I give up a police witness and get caught, my career is ruined. I won't be of any more use to you," Herman tried to reason.

"You need to relax your nerves. You look a little shaken up. Calm down before you wind up peeing on my expensive leather furniture. Then, you will really have a problem," Geno advised him while he laughed. It was amusing to him to see Leftwich act like such a coward.

"I'm almost at the point in my career where I can retire, but you want me to do this risky shit? Damn you, Geno, I guess I have no choice. I will make it happen somehow," Herman promised him.

"That's my boy. That's more like it. That's what I want to hear. I'm glad we could reach an agreement on this matter. Don't worry yourself so much. Don't I always take care of you with a little something every time you deliver as promised for me?" Geno asked him.

"Yes, you do pay me well," Leftwich had to admit.

Over the years, Geno paid Herman a few hundred grand in cold hard cash off the books for his services. The money was tax free and he was free to do what he wanted with the cash. Herman used a good portion of the money to finance his out of town excursions with various teenage boys he met online through dating services and chat rooms.

"I'm glad you can remember that fact. This time will be no different. I'll get what I need from you, and you'll have a nice early Christmas gift to enjoy for your inconvenience," Geno reiterated to him.

"Geno, can I ask why do you need information on this guy?" Herman asked.

"You don't need to be concerned with why I want the information, Herman. Just do what I ask you to do. You'll be thoroughly compensated for your time. That's all you need to be worried about," Geno responded authoritatively.

"Okay, have it your way. I apologize for asking. I'll have the name for you by the end of the week," Herman stated. He gulped down another glass of cognac. The alcohol warmed his insides and put him at ease.

"It's a pleasure doing business with you, Herman. Now that you're finished your drink, get the hell out of my office, you disgusting pedophile. You're lucky I need you from time to time or else I would've turned you in myself to your fellow boys in blue. Vanish from my sight, you piece of shit," Geno stated angrily while he eyed Herman up and down.

"I'm out of here," Herman said before he quickly made his exit.

When Herman outlived his usefulness to him, Geno planned to give him his just due for being a pedophile. He was definitely an expendable resource and easily replaceable. After Herman left his office, Geno still had some more business to conduct. He was glad to have part of his plan already set in motion. Despite his contempt for Herman as a man, he was confident he would get him the information he needed. With that in mind, he placed a call to Jarvis Jackson. He answered on the second ring.

"Geno, I hope you're calling to tell me some good news," Jarvis spoke into the phone.

"We're both rich men already, isn't that good enough news?" Geno joked. Jarvis chuckled as well.

"Man, you are crazy. I can't argue with you about that though because I love being rich and I know you do too. What's up brother?" Jarvis asked.

"I need a favor from you. I have a delicate situation I need handled. You remember how you helped me out with that Joe Conley case a few years back?" I need to do something like that again," Geno replied speaking in code. Jarvis paused briefly to reflect before he responded.

Joe Conley was a long time client and good friend of Geno's who was arrested for an attempted murder charge. He faced a lengthy prison sentence if convicted because it was his third offense. He was also suffering from a brain tumor and didn't have long to live. It was his dying wish to live out his last days as a free man. Geno sympathized with his situation and promised to do whatever he could to grant his wish. Consequently, he got Jarvis to plant the gun used in the shooting in the car of a guy named Harvey Mason, who happened to be a low level street dealer who owed a large debt to Jarvis. Harvey ducked him for several months to avoid having to pay him. Jarvis was going to kill him when he finally caught up to him, but opted to use the trumped up charge instead as his way of settling the debt.

He tipped off one of the dirty cops on his payroll about the gun in Harvey's car. He was arrested shortly thereafter and charged with attempted murder after the police got the ballistics results back on the weapon. Geno agreed to represent Harvey in court pro bono. He managed to get him a plea deal whereby he would have to serve ten years in jail as opposed to the twenty the State offered initially. Joe lived another two years before he passed away and was able to enjoy his last days with his family while an innocent man went to jail for a crime he didn't commit. Geno felt no guilt about what he did. Harvey was just a sacrificial lamb he used to help out a friend in need.

"I sure do remember. I'm sure I can find the right guy to take on that task. You're going to have to give me a few days to make sure he's a perfect fit and it's a done deal," Jarvis replied.

"That's what I like to hear. I'll talk to you soon, my good friend," Geno uttered before he hung up the phone. He sat back in his chair and smiled slyly. All of the pieces for his plan to help Jericho were falling into place like he planned for them to do. Now it was just a waiting game. He poured himself another drink to mellow out and relish the moment. He always seemed to have the right solution to solve all of his and other's life problems. It felt good to be the Boss and to have the world at his feet.

Chapter 4

The steady flow of rain had slacked up as Sal rounded the corner in route to his destination. He walked swiftly down the street accompanied by Cesare. They both stopped and took a moment to put down their umbrellas. They were sharply dressed in custom tailor made suits designed by the Foundation's board member, Giovanni. Nothing personified success more than a man dressed in a sharp suit that exuded confidence in his stride and the way he conversed when he conducted business. Geno and Sal made it their business to give Cesare a crash course on all of the finer points of how to become a solid business man and he was attentive to every lesson. They had a big meeting this morning at the Caprese Foundation office today and they both needed to be in prime form. Sal was nervous, but he maintained a cool external demeanor. Cesare was just as nervous because the whole concept of having a real job was new to him, but he was getting used to the daily routine and responsibilities it required.

Since his life changing jail experience, Cesare had turned over a new leaf. He retired his pipe dream of becoming a rapper and stopped smoking weed altogether. It was a struggle initially to get sober, but he was able to maintain his focus because he now wanted something more for himself than to just spend his time getting high and letting life pass him by. He and Geno were now closer than ever and their relationship had a resounding effect on his new mind state. Cesare now wanted to take a more active role in helping him build the Caprese Foundation. Consequently, Geno appointed Sal to be his mentor and to teach him about the inner workings of the family business.

Sal had his reservations about the assignment initially because of Cesare's history of being unreliable and irresponsible, but, over time, he too noticed a change in Cesare. Since he took him under his wing, he had become more mature and responsible in his actions than Sal had ever seen before. Cesare was finally becoming the man Geno hoped he would become someday. He was proud of his little brother.

Cesare was no longer an aspiring rapper with no long term life plan. He was now enrolled in college at American University pursuing a Bachelor's degree in Computer Science. His ultimate goal was to get his Master's degree in Game Design so he could eventually work alongside Jeremy Whisby in helping him develop CITD into a major player in the video gaming industry alongside companies like EA, Ubisoft, and Nintendo. Since he was a teenager, he was an avid video game player as he spent countless hours high on marijuana in front of his big screen television playing all types of games on the different models of the Playstation that came out over the years. He knew all about the hottest games and he saw this as an asset he could use to help create a meaningful career path that he could excel at if he put in the maximum effort.

When he told Geno the news about his college plans, he was even more excited than Cesare was. He was glad he finally took his advice and became serious about something other than his foolish rap career pipe dream. Geno wanted Cesare to learn more about the inner workings of the organization so he was fully prepared to take his place alongside Geno at the helm of the empire in the very near future. That was his vision when he first started the Foundation. He wanted to build a powerhouse company flanked by his two brothers. However, Silvio's greed and jealousy ruined that plan, but there was still a chance for him and Cesare to make history together.

"Stop walking so slow, Cesare. You move like an old man," Sal uttered while they strolled up the block.

"Ain't nothing old about me, Sal. I just like to take things slow. When I rush and move too fast, I make mistakes. Slow motion is the best motion for me. That's why the ladies love me so much because I like to take my time and give them exactly what they need," Cesare bragged. Sal cackled at his statement.

"You're still wet behind the ears, Cesare. Stick with me and I'll make a man out of you yet," Sal advised his young upstart.

"I hear you, old timer, I hear you. I'm just joking around, Sal, but for real, I'm just anxious to get this day over with as soon as possible," Cesare stated in response.

"Everything will be just fine, Cesare. Just relax and follow my lead," Sal assured his young charge. Truth be told, he was just as eager to get this meeting over and done with because it had weighed on him heavily ever since Geno gave him his marching orders. Whether he was nervous or not, the job had to be done. Geno expected him to deliver as promised. They finally reached their destination and went inside the building.

"How's it going today, Jeremiah?" Sal asked the security guard as he went through the metal detector. Cesare followed right behind him.

"It's going well, Sal. How are you today Cesare?" Jeremiah asked in response.

"I'm good, Big J. I see you're hanging in there," Cesare responded. He placed his cell phone and keys in the plastic tray so they could be processed through the security scanning machine.

"I hit the lottery last night for a few grand so I'm a happy man right now," Jeremiah replied ecstatically. He was a middle aged black man who had worked in the building for over fifteen years. He enjoyed his brief chats with the building tenants as they entered in the morning and left out in the evenings.

"You hit the lottery last night and you're at work today? Man, you're crazy. I would be out with my old lady painting the town right now. You need a day off as hard as you work," Cesare teased him.

"No, sir, I'm not the partying type. That money is going in my savings account. I'll be retiring in two years and then me and my old lady can party all we want to all day and night," he replied.

"You're a wise man, Jeremiah. Have a good day my friend," Sal stated. He patted him on his back and made his way toward the elevator.

"You do the same, Mr. Sal. You take care as well, Cesare," Jeremiah uttered.

They walked over to the elevator. When the doors opened, they got inside and Sal pushed the button for the eleventh floor. The elevator beeped when they reached their desired floor and the doors opened wide like the gates of heaven. They briskly strolled up to the huge double doors of the Foundation and entered. They were greeted by Geno's assistant, Jia. Sal's face lit up when she stood right in front of him. He couldn't even try to hide his physical attraction to her. Cesare had to laugh because Sal was usually calm and composed, but when he was around Jia, he lost his cool and acted out of character. He got a kick out of seeing a hard core gangster like Sal act like a love struck nerd over a woman. He teased him about it on the regular.

"Put your tongue back in your mouth, Sal. You're looking thirsty," Cesare joked.

"She wants me. She's just doesn't know how to deal with a real man like me yet. Ain't that right doll face?" Sal asked her.

"Hello, Mr. Sal. Hello, Cesare. How are you gentleman doing today?" Jia spoke in her most professional tone. She totally ignored Sal's weak attempt to flirt with her.

"Hello, Jia, don't pay Sal any mind. He's just being Sal," Cesare interjected.

"Hey there, gorgeous, you're looking stunning in that dress today. How about you finally let me take you out for dinner so I can show you a good time tonight?" Sal asked suggestively.

Jia could feel Sal's eyes all over her, but she did her best to ignore his obvious sexual advances toward her no matter how much they made her want to throw up in her mouth. She had no choice because he was Geno's best friend and business partner. If she wanted to keep her job, she had to have thick skin and learn how to deal with him wisely.

"I don't think my boyfriend would like that idea," she suggested. Truth be told, she didn't have a steady guy in her life, but that wasn't Sal's business to know. Besides, she only had eyes for Geno even though he was out of her reach.

"You tell him he's one lucky son of a gun," Sal joked.

"I certainly will tell him. On another note, the board room is all set up for your meeting today," Jia informed him.

"Thanks, Jia. You're a sweetheart," he stated with a smile. He shook his head when she walked past him on the way to her office because he wanted her badly. He turned all the way around to get one last glance at her backside. He fantasized about what he could do with her in the bedroom if she were his, but then he snapped back to reality because he had business to handle. He made his way to the board room and turned on the light. He was relieved they were early and the first ones there. That meant he and Cesare still had a brief moment to get themselves mentally prepared for the meeting.

"You're dreaming if you think you're getting with her, Sal," Cesare butted in to interrupt his fantasy.

"I'll get her one day. You can bet the house on that. Never mind Jia, are you ready for this meeting?" Sal asked him.

"I'm as ready as I'll ever be," Cesare stated honestly.

When the Caprese Foundation was established, it was set up to consist of eleven members. Each member was given an equal vote in all decisions made by the board. Geno, of course, was the chairman of the board and he controlled a fifty percent share of the corporation. Even though Silvio was a member of the board, and owned five shares, he never attended any of its meetings or voted on any issues. He gave Geno his proxy to act on his behalf. Cesare wasn't a board member, but he received a monthly stipend from Geno out of his share of the profits because he felt he was entitled to it as a member of the Caprese family. Cesare happily received his generous allotment and didn't complain one bit. Sal was the next largest shareholder at ten percent. He was given this large of a percentage due to his loyalty to Geno over the years. Milton and Jarvis Jackson each owned a five percent share of the Foundation.

The other twenty five percent of the Foundation was split equally amongst the other six board members. They included Sam Braxton, the president of Mahogany Bank, the largest African American owned bank on the East Coast and where the Foundation laundered a significant amount of its dirty money, Charles Proctor, the head of the industrial real estate development firm, Proctor Realty, Giovanni Giordano, owner of Giordano Fashions, Tony Martin, a well respected sports agent who represented several top NBA and NFL athletes, Edgar Phillips, the head of Phillips Home Improvement, a regional chain of home improvement stores, and Jonas Berkovitz, a well respected Jewish philanthropist who owned a wide array of successful businesses across the city. Berkovitz was also an old acquaintance of Leonardo Caprese who had ties to the old school Jewish Mafia.

Geno wisely chose all of the board members because of their particular business expertise and their level of respect in the legitimate business community. He wanted a well rounded group of solid business men from different walks of life to ensure the Foundation would have a diversified portfolio of business interests that it chose to invest in. He also had to make sure they were men whom he could trust or that feared him. He demanded the utmost loyalty from his board. They knew and understood that any disloyalty or betrayal of the Foundation would lead to death. Geno, thanks to his resourceful and thorough private detective, John Lucci, had dirt on all of them which he wouldn't hesitate to use to destroy them professionally and on a personal level if necessary to maintain control of his organization.

As the members of the board filtered into the conference room, Sal sat in the seat normally reserved for Geno and greeted them all one by one. Cesare sat down beside him. He had butterflies in his stomach. Sal's calm outward demeanor masked the bundle of nerves he felt inside. Geno was in court today working on a big case and asked him to step in to run the meeting on his behalf. This was unfamiliar territory for Sal because he was used to sitting at Geno's side and being a silent observer while he led the meetings. He was comfortable playing the second man in charge, but Geno had expressed to him recently he wanted him to be more assertive in assuming more leadership duties to lighten his own responsibilities.

Geno wanted Sal to show him he made a wise choice in placing so much trust in him. Today was his chance to show and prove he had what it took to do the job if Geno needed him to step up to the plate temporarily to fill his shoes. He gave Sal a specific task to accomplish today he was sure the board wouldn't like, but it was his job to make it happen and deliver as instructed.

"Hello, gentleman, I think we can finally call this meeting to order because it looks like everyone is here. I'm glad you all could make it in for this spur of the moment meeting today. We just have one important item to discuss. I promise not to take up too much of your time because I know you all have busy schedules," Sal promised.

"Hey, where's Geno? He's the chairman of the board. Shouldn't he be here to run this meeting?" Jonas interjected in his gruff voice. He never liked Sal not because of anything he did, but because of a beef he had with Sal's father, Alfonso, from their days of running the streets in New York in the 1960's. They were bitter enemies for years, but Leonardo, who happened to be friends with both, served as a peace maker between the two of them. Sal was the splitting image of his father and just to see his face brought back bad memories for Jonas. Sal paid his little verbal jabs no mind and simply dismissed him as an old school gangster still trying to hold on to his reputation from the past. Since Geno respected Jonas enough to make him a board member, he did his best to keep the peace with him.

"What's he doing here? He's not a board member!" Tony Martin stated vehemently in reference to Cesare.

"Geno had other business to tend to today so he asked me to step in for him. Cesare is here because he's a Caprese and has a right to be here. Is that a problem for anyone? If it is, please let it be known. I will be sure to convey your issues to Geno," Sal stated rather directly and to the point. He wanted to make it clear to all of the board members he acted with the full support of Geno in whatever business he handled in his absence.

"There's no problem at all, Sal," Giovanni chimed in.

"It doesn't matter to me," Charles added.

"Let's get to it, then," Sam suggested.

"Well, as you all are aware, since Silvio has disappeared and has never been an active member of the board, Geno thought it was wise at this time we fill his seat on the board with a new member. He wants to appoint a member who will actually be a voting member and active in our decision making process. He is proposing that we welcome Cesare as that new member," Sal stated rather directly. He glanced in Milton and Jarvis' direction for a vote of confidence. They both nodded their heads in affirmation to let him know they had his back.

"Are you serious? This has to be a joke, right?" Jonas blurted out.

"This kid has no business experience at all. What is Geno thinking about?" Sam added. Several other board members also chimed in to express their displeasure with Geno's selection.

"Do you see a smile on my face? Does it look like I'm joking? Geno would like your full support of his decision and would be extremely disappointed in anyone who opposes his selection. He wants us to put this to a vote," Sal stated rather authoritatively. There were tight faces and mean mugs throughout the room. Before a vote was taken, Cesare rose to his feet and placed his hand on Sal's shoulder.

"Sal, I want to have a chance to address the board before a vote is taken. Since I'm here, who is better to speak on my behalf to you all? Let me start off by saying I can understand your being hesitant about accepting me on the board because I don't have anywhere near the level of business expertise that any of you gentleman do. This is a fact that can't be ignored. I also don't want you to vote for me because Geno is my brother. I'm my own man with my own mind. I'm eager to learn all I can from each and every one of you if you give me a chance. What I want to add to this board is a new set of eyes that reflects the pulse of the younger generation. You all have seen how much money ventures like CITD have generated off of video games and that's why I chose to get my degree in this area of study so I can help that branch of the company grow even more. However, I don't plan to stop there. Giovanni, you're a genius in the fashion industry, but how about if you had a young pair of eyes like mine to help you come up with a Caprese clothing line for the urban youth that could generate millions of dollars like companies such as Echo and Sean John? Tony, I can see us working together to get some of those professional athletes you represent to use their popularity to advertise the clothing line and some other innovative products I have in mind like maybe our own line of headphones. Dr. Dre and 50 Cent are making a ton of money off of them. It's these kinds of innovative ideas that I want to help us develop and bring into fruition to expand the Foundation's portfolio. I want to help take this organization to the next level and make us all even richer. If you let me be a part of this board, I can promise you, it's a decision you will not live to regret," he passionately pleaded his case.

Cesare wanted to be accepted for who he was and what he could contribute and not just because he was Geno's younger brother. He eloquently expressed his intentions to the board and his remarks appeared to be well received. It was clear he had done some research and didn't just speak off the cuff. Sal was impressed with how well Cesare was able to represent himself. He noticed the positive body language and head nods Cesare received from several of the other board members after he spoke his mind. Cesare and Sal got up from the table and exited the room for a few minutes to let the other board members talk among themselves.

"How did I do, Sal?" Cesare asked eagerly.

"You kicked ass in there, Cesare. I'm proud of you man. You surprised me for sure. I can't wait to tell Geno how well you did. Let's wrap this up.

They've had enough time to talk," Sal stated calmly.

"I'll follow your lead," Cesare said. They walked back into the board room and sat back down in their seats at the head of the table.

"I don't think there is much more to say at this point. Let's all cast our vote. I'll start things off. I vote in favor of allowing Cesare to be a board member," Sal stated with conviction.

Within minutes, they had a final tally of the votes. It was decided by an 8 to 2 member vote to allow Cesare to join the board. The only two dissenting votes were from Sam Braxton and Jonas Berkovitz, but they didn't matter. Geno got what he wanted and would be pleased. His younger brother would be standing right beside him along his journey to the top of the corporate world. Sal was also sure he would earn stripes for himself with Geno for being able to pull this off without a hitch in his absence. He was confident he would be rewarded royally for his efforts. He adjourned the meeting and everyone went their separate ways. He and Cesare left out to celebrate their successful meeting at Maggie's. The future for the Caprese Foundation looked bright.

Chapter 5

Elias Knox got up every morning at the crack of dawn to fix himself his morning cup of hot coffee, two hard fried eggs, and two slices of buttered toast with grape jelly. He followed this same pattern for over thirty years as a mail handler for the United States Postal Service and still carried on the tradition even though he had been retired for almost five years. In his mid fifties, he stood a towering six feet and six inches tall and weighed close to two hundred and fifty pounds. He had a head full of gray hair and all of the body aches and pains which came along with being a middle-aged Black man in America who had worked hard for so many years.

In his younger days, Elias was the star forward on his high school basketball team. He even played two years of college basketball on a full athletic scholarship at Morgan State University before he suffered an acute Achilles tendon rupture while playing a pickup game in the summer time. The injury ended his playing days and left him with a nagging limp. He used a cane for support to help him when he walked. With his hoop dreams over, he dropped out of school in the middle of his junior year and went through a period of depression. When he came out of his funk, he was hit with a stroke of good luck when an old college friend who worked at the post office told him about a job opening and helped him land the job. Elias was able to earn a decent enough salary to be able to eventually buy a beautiful two story home in East Baltimore. He shared the home with his wife, Lindsay, and his son, Elias II, who was born a year after they moved in.

Sadly, Lindsay, his wife of almost thirty years, passed away three years ago from a heart attack. Her death came as a surprise to everyone because she had always been a woman with no major medical problems. Since her death, Elias lived his life in virtual solitude from the outside world. He was crushed that he lost his soul mate. He and Lindsay were high school sweethearts and virtually inseparable. She was the only woman he had ever truly loved and when she died, he had no desire to either date or remarry. No woman could ever occupy the special place she held in his heart. Their bond was eternal and never to be broken, not even by death. He longed for the day he would see her again in the Hereafter. Life without her was simply a state of dismal abyss for Elias.

Even though he had no desire to remarry, Elias was still a man with physical needs. Whenever he was in the mood for female companionship, he would hop in his car and ride down to the Garrison Boulevard area in Northwest Baltimore and find himself a prostitute to fulfill his sexual desires. It was his way of temporarily blocking out the emotional pain he felt inside since Lindsay's death. He was arrested several times for soliciting prostitutes, but it didn't matter to him because he felt like he didn't have much to live for anyway without Lindsay. He simply paid the fines when he went to court.

In addition to the periodic company he got from hookers, Tanqueray gin also comforted him in his hours of need. He was a social drinker for most of his life, but was now a full-fledged alcoholic. He drank at least a fifth per day and it drastically changed his behavior for the worst. He was no longer the mild mannered, family man he had been for years. He was now a mean drunk, prone to violent mood swings when he was under the influence.

His son, Elias II, graduated from high school and moved to Virginia to attend college at Hampton University. He graduated with a Doctorate in Physical Therapy and currently operated his own independent practice in the Norfolk area. He lived there with his wife and two young daughters. He and his father used to have a close relationship before his mother's death, but once his father began to drink heavily, they drifted apart. His unpredictable behavior made it hard to be around him for long periods of time.

When he was drunk, his father was prone to violent outbursts he later regretted once he sobered up. Elias II was forced to defend himself countless times from these violent attacks whenever he would come to visit his father. He was both saddened and embarrassed by his behavior and didn't want his children to witness their grandfather in such a state so he kept them away from him. He understood his father's pain over his mother's death and just prayed he would one day get help for his drinking problem so he would have a chance to build a close relationship with his grandchildren. Until he did, he kept his distance from his father and only called him on occasion just to check on him.

The only hobby Elias had outside of chasing hookers and drinking alcohol was that he loved to go to the race track. His best friend from his days working at the post office, Jerry, came by on Thursdays and they would go to Pimlico Race Course to bet on the horses. Jerry was an alcoholic as well. The two of them enabled each other's addictive behavior. They would get into physical fights one day and then be the best of friends the next. Many times, they would both experience blackouts and not even remember what they fought about the night before. Elias rarely won when he bet, but he got an adrenaline rush from watching the horses make a mad dash to the finish line.

On this particular morning, Elias sat at the kitchen table and read the newspaper while he ate his breakfast and drank a cup of coffee spiked with a double shot of Tanqueray gin. When he was done eating his breakfast and browsing through the newspaper, he grabbed his cane which was next to his chair. He steadied himself with his hand on the table as he rose to his feet. It was trash day and he had to set his garbage cans out by the curb so they could be emptied. He headed toward his kitchen door outside to the rear of his house. He gingerly walked down the worn wooden stairs toward his garage. He kept his trash cans inside of the garage until trash day because if he left them out in the alley, stray dogs in the neighborhood would ransack his trash and make a mess he would have to clean up. When he reached the garage, he unhooked the latch on the door and went inside to retrieve the trash cans. As he dragged them back to the door to make his way out to the alley, he was startled when he was greeted by two gun wielding men who blocked his path.

"Hey, hold on now! What the hell is this? I don't have any money. I'm just a poor old man living here alone. Please don't shoot me," Elias begged.

"We're not going to shoot you, old man, so just relax. You need to come with us," the tall young, African American male stated firmly. He stepped to the side to make room for Elias to walk by him, but Elias remained still frozen with fear.

"Come with you where? I'm just a drunk old man with a bad leg. What do you want with me?" Elias asked.

"Don't ask too many questions. Just come with us. If you cooperate, you will have no worries. Nobody is going to hurt you. I give you my word. Now get in the damn van!" the second man yelled at him with his gun pointed at Elias's head. He was a Caucasian male who looked to be significantly older than his taller partner in crime. His physical presence wasn't as imposing as his partner's was, but the gun in his hand could do more than enough damage to get his point across.

"I ain't going nowhere with you punks. Get the hell off of my property before I call the police!" Elias threatened. He had a burst of liquid courage and decided to stand his ground. He felt like he had nothing to lose.

"Have it your way, Pops!" the younger man stated reluctantly. He didn't want to hurt Elias, but his defiant stance left him no choice. He aggressively moved forward and grabbed Elias's arm. When Elias tried to pull away from him, he used his foot to kick him in his bad leg. The impact of the blow forced Elias to double over in pain.

"You must think you're one hell of a tough guy to beat up on an old man, huh? If I was twenty years younger, I would kick your ass!" Elias threatened.

Before the young man could respond, his accomplice joined in on the fracas and clocked Elias over the head with his gun. He fell to the ground. The blow knocked him out cold. The younger thug bent down to check his pulse. He was relieved to discover he was still alive. The two men hovered over him as they tried to figure out their next move.

"What the hell did you do that for, Arturo?" the younger thug asked.

"He was asking for it, Bunchy. He should've just kept his mouth closed and did as we told him to do," he replied.

"Since you knocked him out cold, go get the rope and duct tape so we can take him to the meeting spot," Bunchy ordered him.

"I'll be right back," Arturo stated before he exited the garage. He returned shortly with the supplies. The two men tied Elias' arms behind his back and duct taped his mouth shut. They lifted him up off the ground and carried him out to the van they had parked in the alley. They looked around in all directions to ensure there were no witnesses. Elias was tossed on the cold floor in the empty van like a sack of potatoes. Bunchy sat in the back with Elias. Arturo hopped in the driver's seat and pulled off slowly. About thirty minutes later, they reached their destination. Arturo jumped out of the van and opened up the rear door. He helped Bunchy carry Elias' limp body inside. Once that was done, Bunchy pulled out of his phone to send his Boss a text message to inform him the mission was accomplished. They waited for further instructions.

Chapter 6

Lincoln's mood currently could best be described as manic. He paced back and forth across the floor of his father's home study. He couldn't seem to keep still for a second. His pupils were dilated and beads of sweat formed on his forehead. His jittery nerves were another obvious sign he was under the influence of some type of illicit substance. When he opened up his mouth and spoke, Geno truly realized he wasn't playing with a full deck and not in his right mind. He rambled on like a mad lunatic endlessly without taking a pause.

"That tramp is lying, Geno. You saw it for yourself when she got on the stand. You could tell she was faking with all of those tears. That was an award winning performance. She wanted it just as much as I did. I didn't have to force her to do a thing. She just wants our money. She had this whole thing planned to set me up. Look at me...do I look like the kind of guy who has to force a woman to have sex with him?" Lincoln asked rhetorically. Humility was certainly not his strong suit.

Geno just looked at him with a blank stare on his face. He wanted to slap the taste out of his mouth to get him to shut up. Lincoln's father was embarrassed by his erratic behavior. On the surface, Lincoln's assumption was correct because most women he encountered did find him attractive. He was tall, with a muscular physique. He had a set of dreamy blue eyes that would put any woman in a trance if she gazed at them for too long. He resembled the late actor Paul Walker with his movie star good looks. However, with all of his appealing physical attributes, he left a lot to be desired in the personality department. Lincoln had the social skills of a Neanderthal. He embodied the image of the spoiled college kid who grew up with a sense of social entitlement and privilege. He was the antithesis of what Geno represented which was why just the sound of his voice irked him so.

"Kid, you know sometimes a fool doesn't know he is a fool even if you tell him so. Being silent is something you need start practicing," Geno stated sarcastically.

"What do you mean?" Lincoln asked. He obviously missed Geno's point.

"Never mind, kid, it wasn't mean for you to understand. Judge, I'll take another glass of

Hennessy please. I'm going to need it," Geno uttered.

The Judge walked over to the bar and poured them both a drink. He didn't even bother to ask Lincoln if he wanted something to drink because it didn't matter. He was just as perturbed with him as Geno was. Lincoln wasn't even smart enough to realize Geno had just insulted him to his face with his comment. He simply continued on with his manic rant.

"Lincoln, sometimes I have to ask myself was I drinking too much when I got your mother pregnant because your level of stupidity befuddles me sometimes," the Judge stated, clearly agitated with his wayward offspring.

The look on Geno's face as he sipped on his drink was that of a man who was mentally drained. He wasn't the kind of man to bite his tongue normally, but he also understood sometimes it was wiser to take a moment of silence before he spoke in certain situations because his first response would likely be something said out of anger that he couldn't take back. He envisioned himself strangling the life out of Lincoln for being so arrogant and cocky.

No matter how much he disliked a client personally, he always tried to be professional. However, Lincoln Bukowski pushed his patience to the limit. He was way past his limit in dealing with

Lincoln's idiotic, immature behavior. Things didn't go well for him today in court which was something that happened rarely to such a brilliant legal mind as his. No matter how well prepared he was to do battle in the courtroom, no attorney could always account for the counterproductive behavior of his client which made his job harder. Lincoln's recent antics were a perfect example of such a situation.

Lincoln Bukowski was a twenty something year old college student at the University of Maryland who was charged with sexually assaulting a female student at a college fraternity party. To add insult to injury, the alleged victim claimed he slipped the date rape drug, Rohypnol, into her drink before he assaulted her. As a result, in addition to the rape charge, he also faced a possession with intent to distribute a controlled dangerous substance charge. It was reported by several witnesses at the party that he sold drugs on the campus. When they searched his dorm room, the police found a significant amount of Rohypnol, as well as Ecstasy pills, and small bags of marijuana inside of his private area. All of the evidence stacked against Lincoln Bukowski made the case an uphill battle for Geno to overcome, but he was up for the challenge.

Geno rarely took on cases involving rape or anything of a sexual nature because he saw men who preyed upon women as cowards. He had no respect for them at all and rightfully so. However, in this instance, he made an exception because of the benefits he could reap if he were able to win the case. Lincoln happened to be the son of The Honorable Lance Bukowski, a Maryland State Circuit Court judge.

Judge Bukowski was known for being firm but fair in his court rulings. He was a major player in political and business circles as well. Geno had tried numerous cases in his courtroom with much success over the years. They also had conversed casually on numerous occasions at various social mixers reserved strictly for Maryland's socially elite upper class.

When it hit the news about his son's arrest, Judge Bukowski knew Geno was the right man to call to get his son out of this mess. He needed a lawyer to do damage control and to quell the media fiasco that would surely follow. Ever since he was a teenager, Lincoln stayed in trouble in school or with the law. He had a history of school suspensions for fighting or being disruptive in class. He had a few juvenile arrests for petty charges like marijuana possession or shoplifting. Those arrests were either dismissed or warranted nothing more than probation for him, but this time around, Lincoln was looking at a long stretch in the state penitentiary if he was convicted.

To get him out of this mess, the Judge needed a lawyer with the necessary legal resources at his disposal to give his son the best possible legal defense. He would spare no expense to preserve his highly respected family name from public shame and ridicule. He had worked hard to build up a solid reputation and would be damned if he let his son's foolish behavior further tarnish his image in the public.

Geno took the case because he saw it as a win win situation for him. If he were able to get Lincoln off on the charges or at least negotiate an amenable plea bargain, Judge Bukowski would be indebted to him and it would be a debt he would surely cash in on at the appropriate time in the future. However, with the way the case had gone so far, Geno almost felt he may have bit off more than he could chew.

Thus far during the trial, the prosecutor had laid out a wealth of circumstantial evidence against Lincoln. Geno came out with both guns blazing and did his best to call into question all of the evidence and testimony presented by the State. He believed his clever cross examination of the State's witnesses and the testimony from his own legal experts about the validity of the DNA evidence presented had been solid enough to begin to plant a reasonable doubt in the minds of the jurors. For every student who testified Lincoln was a drug dealer on the campus, he found just as many to attest to him being a straight A student of upstanding character who would never indulge in such illegal acts. He paid several female students to attest to Lincoln being nothing less than a perfect gentleman while in their presence. He had several of the Judge's colleagues to testify on Lincoln's behalf as character witnesses. It appeared to Geno that the jury was swayed by his efforts. They seemed to buy into the idea that Lincoln was a clean cut college boy from a rich family who was being framed by his accuser in an attempt to extort money from his family.

The tide in the case began to shift when the alleged victim took the stand and testified in detail about what happened to her. Geno was torn because he could tell she told the truth when she described how she was violated. He had developed an uncanny ability to be able to read a person's body language and emotional reactions while on the witness stand after having practiced law for so many years. When he heard her describe how she remembered first having a drink with Lincoln at the party and then waking up in bed nude with him the next day, it made his blood boil. He thought about Gianna and what he would do to any young punk like Lincoln who ever tried to take advantage of her in the same manner.

However, despite his personal feelings, he reminded himself he had a job to do. Consequently, he did what he did best and went on the attack by calling into question the young lady's character when he cross examined her. John Lucci was able to discover the young lady had a history of drug abuse and had been to drug rehab several times in her teenage years. He was also able to find several old boyfriends who testified about how she liked to party a lot and who suggested she was promiscuous. His aim was to suggest that both the sexual intercourse between Lincoln and the alleged victim and the drug use were consensual. He did a good job in conveying this message to the juror. However, he felt like a total jerk for further traumatizing the young lady, but it had to be done. A feeling of remorse overcame him when he watched her step off the witness stand in such a fragile emotional state after she answered his probing questions.

Even though his defense strategies were well executed and he felt pretty good about winning the case, what had him hot currently was that after all of the clever legal maneuvering he had done to try and win the case thus far, Lincoln did just as much to sabotage his efforts. In spite of his specific directions to Lincoln not to make any statements to the press, he decided to go against Geno's wishes anyway. Geno just found out Lincoln went on the largest local talk radio show in Baltimore City the night before to profess his innocence and to further lambast his alleged victim. He went on a tirade in an attempt to portray himself as the victim. He alleged the entire case was a conspiracy on the young lady's part to attempt to extort money from his family.

When he made his allegation, the phone lines at the radio station lit up with calls from members of various women's rights groups and domestic violence advocates, as well as sexual assault victims, who called in to rake him over the coals for some of the inflammatory statements he made. There were protesters outside of the courthouse when he entered the court this morning and when he left out at the end of the day. Geno briskly strolled by them all, flanked by Lincoln and his father, without making a statement to the press. The damage was already done and to try and defend Lincoln's actions would just add insult to injury. He chose to keep his battle tactics in the courtroom instead of trying this case in the media. The courtroom was an arena where he was known to work miracles in the murkiest of legal situations.

"Judge, we both can see clearly your son is a scumbag and he raped this girl. The facts speak for themselves. He deserves to have his balls cut off and to spend the rest of his life in jail being some big burly prisoner's girlfriend. However, I will be frank with you because I think you deserve my honesty. I took this case because I respect you as a man and you have always been fair with me whenever I presented a case in your courtroom. This was a courtesy and favor to you despite my personal contempt for this little prick. When I get him acquitted or at least a more than fair plea deal, I hope you understand you will be in my debt. I may call on you someday to repay this debt and I expect you to do the honorable thing and act accordingly. With that being said, this is my last warning to you and young Lincoln. From here on out, he better keep his mouth shut and not say a word to the press or I give you my word, I will personally see to it he gets the just punishment he deserves for ruining this young lady's life," Geno promised them. He sat back calmly in his seat and finished off the last of his drink. He glanced down at his cell phone and noticed he had received a text message. He lifted up the phone to read the message and smiled as he placed the phone back on his hip.

"Dad, are you going to just stand there and let him talk to you like that? He works for us. Put him in his place!" Lincoln demanded.

Geno chuckled at the thought of the Judge being able to reprimand him for what he just said. It was clear to him Lincoln had no clue who he was and how much power he wielded in the City. He surely thought Geno was just another high priced attorney and not a deadly gangster who could have him killed before the night was over if he chose to do so.

"Lincoln, shut your mouth! You talk too much as it is. Geno you won't have any more problems from him or I will kick his ass myself. I give you my word," Judge Bukowski promised. He knew all about Geno's reputation and chose to tread lightly with the way he addressed him. He was a powerful man in his own right, but Geno represented a different level of power that was out of his league. Lincoln simply stood silently not knowing what to think or say.

"Kid, let me try to break this down so you can understand me clearly. If you want to go to jail, I can just walk away from this case and let your father hire another attorney. I promise you won't find another one who can make things happen like I can. However, if you want to remain free, then follow my lead. When I'm done working my magic, I'm going to work out a deal where you won't do a day in jail, but be on house arrest if you cop a plea to a lesser charge. You might have to admit you have a drug problem and enroll in a drug treatment program. Now you tell me, how does that sound?" Geno asked. He awaited Lincoln's response.

"I can't argue with that at all. I just want this all to be over and done with for good. Thank you, Geno. I apologize for the stupid things I did," Lincoln stated. He had calmed down quite a bit. His high appeared to be wearing off. He also realized that to be on house arrest in his father's mansion sounded a lot better than possibly going to jail and living with hardened criminals for years not knowing if he would live to see another day.

"I'm glad we could reach an understanding. I appreciate your hospitality, but I have to cut this meeting short. I have other business to tend to tonight. I will see you gentleman bright and early tomorrow morning. I can show myself out," Geno stated in a more relaxed mood than when he originally arrived. He got up from his seat and walked right past Lincoln, as though he wasn't even in the room. He walked over to the Judge and shook his hand before he exited the study.

When Geno made it out of the mansion to his car, his driver, Clay, opened the rear passenger door to his Mercedes-Maybach S600 so he could get inside. The Maybach was the newest toy Geno added to his collection of expensive European vehicles. He paid a hefty amount of money to have it bulletproofed for his safety. He no longer drove around town alone, but instead always had a team of armed security guards who followed closely behind him in a second vehicle for his protection. Since he exterminated Nesta and his crew and left little question he was the King of the underworld in Baltimore, he knew he had a target on his back. Geno thought it was wise for him to be extra cautious than to be cocky about his lofty status in the streets because that was the easiest way to get caught out of pocket by your enemy. There would be hell to pay if anything happened to him or any member of his family.

"I hope everything went well, Geno. Am I taking you home now?" Clay asked, as he maneuvered the car down the winding driveway of the Judge's estate grounds toward the road.

"Yes, everything went well, Clay. Thanks for asking, kid. I'm not going home just yet. We have one more stop to make before I call it a night. I swear my days never seem to end. Sometimes it sucks being the Boss," Geno confessed to express his level of exhaustion. He gave Clay the address to where they were headed.

"Well, Geno, you know that saying heavy is the head that wears the crown? It describes you perfectly. I can think of many men out here who would give their lives or even take lives to be in your shoes, but they're just not equip for the job. From what I've seen since I've worked for you is that you run a tight ship and your men respect you wholeheartedly. They are all loyal to you. You were born to be a leader. I know you can handle anything that comes your way, tired or not," Clay responded rather honestly.

Clay idolized Geno and studied his every movement and action. As his driver, he got a firsthand look at the inner workings of the life of a crime boss and philanthropist. It was an educational experience better than any he could receive from a college professor with numerous advanced degrees. They might be able to teach him the theories behind corporate America's foundation, but Geno was the living manifestation of the ultimate businessman who put them into practice in a masterful manner.

"You know, to be so young, you're a pretty smart guy, Clay. I like the fact you're humble and open to learning from me. I'm glad I brought you into the family. You stick with me and I can see big things coming up for you in the future," Geno stated.

Geno reminisced about how when he met Clay he was the parking attendant at the garage where he parked his car in downtown Baltimore whenever he had a case at the courthouse. In their brief conversations, Geno learned he was enrolled in college part-time, but he also dabbled with selling small quantities of weed on the side to supplement his income. Geno saw he had potential and felt he could use another young energetic soldier in his crew. When he offered him the job to be his personal driver, Clay jumped at the opportunity to work for such a powerful and influential person. They developed a very cordial relationship over time and Clay felt comfortable enough to go to Geno for advice about various life situations. He viewed him like an uncle and respected his opinion and guidance.

"I'm not going anywhere, Geno. I appreciate you taking a chance on me by giving me a job. I won't let you down. If you need me to do anything else besides drive you around, I'm up for the task. I'm always ready to put in some work so I can prove to you my worth," Clay replied to express his gratitude and ambition.

"Slow your roll, Clay. In due time, you will get your chance to move up in the family. For now, just enjoy the easy work while you get paid well," Geno advised him.

He liked the hunger and fearlessness he saw in Clay. He saw him as a diamond in the rough he could mold in his own image in time. He definitely planned to make a position for him within the organization in the near future. He sat back to fully relax in the soft leather seats and closed his eyes to rest briefly until he reached his destination. He couldn't wait until he was done with all of his daily tasks so he could make it home before his children went to bed. To see them at the end of a long, stressful day reminded him why he did the things he did to be successful. It was all for them.

Chapter 7

Jericho hadn't felt this uncomfortable and on edge in quite some time. His heart rate was elevated due to the anxiety he felt inside. He told himself over and over again he needed to calm down so he could focus his full attention on his current target. It had been a minute since his last kill and he felt out of practice. Ever since the whole Shavon rape incident occurred, he told Gutta he didn't want to take any new contracts until this situation was resolved because he knew he would be distracted and not on his A game. If he wasn't at his best, it would leave room for him to make a mistake or miscalculated judgment which could either cost him his life or his freedom.

Gutta understood his position and respected him for it because he knew how much Shavon meant to him. She was the only person outside of

Nina and himself that Jericho loved. It was only fitting he put his full focus into helping her heal from the brutal rape she experienced. While Jericho tended to Shavon and Nina's needs, he farmed out jobs to other qualified hit men he had trained over the years. None of them were as thorough and flawless with their work as Jericho was, but they were efficient enough to hold him down until Jericho was back on board.

Jericho's primary focus and concern currently had been to make sure Shavon got the help she needed to address her mental health issues. He didn't know what he would do with himself if she didn't get better soon. He needed her to be whole again. To see her in such a broken state day had his mind totally messed up. He was beyond frustrated. He was mad at the world and needed an outlet to release his frustration. He was going out of his mind living in isolation. He felt trapped having to stay out in the middle of nowhere until this entire ordeal was resolved. He was born and raised in the city and not well suited for the rural environment. Jericho had confidence in the fact Geno would keep his word and come through for him, but his patience was running thin. If he didn't hear from him soon, he planned to take matters into his own hands.

The frustration Jericho felt made him feel powerless. He yearned to feel the rush he got when he eliminated a target. He was in his comfort zone when he stalked his prey until his intended target was lined up perfectly for him to go in for the kill. It was something about the idea of death that soothed Jericho's mind and brought a sense of calm over his entire being. He had a dark, sinister side to him that would make for a dream case study for any psychotherapist intrigued enough to want to look inside the mind of a trained killing machine to see what made him tick.

Without his favorite outlet in his life right now, he was on the verge of losing his mind. If he wasn't sharp mentally, then he would be of no use to Shavon or Nina. For his own sanity, he had to make the tough decision to get back to doing what he did best if he wanted to get back to being his regular self. Consequently, he told Gutta he needed an assignment to complete to get his mind right. Those words were music to Gutta's ears because even though he was empathetic to Jericho's situation with Shavon and Nina, he needed his partner in crime back. He had the perfect job in mind for him that he was sure would help Jericho regain his prime form. He gave Jericho the entire rundown on his next victim and he was overly eager to get to work. Just the thought of carrying out the hit made him feel invigorated.

Jericho's target for his current mission was a man named Joseph Balker. He was an ex-police officer from Hampton, Virginia who was involved in an altercation with an unarmed fifteen year old

Black honor roll high school student named Noel Atkins which resulted in the young man's tragic death. Balker alleged he was riding by in his squad car on the day of the incident when he witnessed Noel and another young man in the process of conducting what he thought was a drug transaction on a street corner. According to his version of the events that led up to the shooting, Balker maintained that the two young men took off running in separate directions when he pulled his squad car in front of them to arrest them. He said he instantly radioed for backup and hopped out of the car to pursue them on foot. The other young man got away because he was a much faster runner than Noel.

He stated that when he finally caught up to Noel in an alley a few blocks away, he made an attempt to place him under arrest, but Noel resisted and a fight between the two of them ensued. During the scuffle, Balker contended that Noel reached for his gun and it went off three times. The first bullet hit up against the brick wall of the building behind them while the other two bullets hit Noel twice in the chest and he fell to the ground.

Balker stated he was unclear as to which one of them fired the fatal shots because both of their hands were wrapped around the gun at the same time. Noel was taken to the hospital where he died two days later as a result of his injuries. After an internal police investigation, no charges were filed against Balker. There were no drugs found anywhere near the crime scene or on Noel or the other young man, who was apprehended a few blocks away by another officer.

Even though he was in the clear, Balker resigned from his position on the police force because after all of the recent shooting incidents and other deaths nationwide which involved White police officers and members of the African American community, he feared for his safety if he were to return to the job. As a result, he sold his house and relocated to another city in an attempt to start a new life. With over twenty-five years of total service on several different police forces across the country, he had a good amount of money saved up in his pension fund to start a new life elsewhere without having to struggle financially. Meanwhile, Noel's mother was forced to bear the emotional pain of her son's death while she continued to live in poverty.

The Black community in Hampton was outraged that another young Black male died in an incident involving a White police officer with no legal repercussions for the officer's actions. Even though they demanded Balker be arrested for Noel's death, their cries went unheard. Noel had no history of being involved with drugs or any illegal activities. The other young man involved in the incident had a few minor arrests for charges like petty theft and loitering, but no charges related to either drug dealing or CDS possession.

Noel was described by members of the community as a smart, respectful young man who attended church every Sunday and pretty much stayed to himself. His friends said he had plans to go to college and to one day become a surgeon like Dr. Ben Carson. However, his dream would never come to fruition. Instead, Noel became another statistic. The blood stained concrete where his lifeless body lay was just another memory of another young Black life with limitless potential lost at the hands of law enforcement. Another Black mother was forced to bury her child prematurely. The pain and frustration further scarred and damaged an already disenfranchised neighborhood and left the community primed for a social revolt to occur like what happened in Baltimore after the death of Freddie Gray.

Community members familiar with Officer Balker reported he had a history of harassing young Black men in the neighborhood just because of their race. There were several other complaints filed against him in the past for assault and brutality, but none of them resulted in any disciplinary action against him. With his reputation in the Hampton community, it was no wonder that Noel and his friend took off running when Balker approached them. The community rallied together and protested the tragedy. The incident made national headlines in both the print media and on every television news outlet across the country.

When Gutta saw the story on the news, he became furious. After the Trayvon Martin and Mike Brown incidents, as well as all of the many racial injustices he witnessed coming up in the 1960's and 1970's, he had enough and decided if law enforcement wouldn't give Black folks justice, he would administer some street justice on his own. He planned to make an example out of Joseph Balker to send a clear message to White America that the lives of young Black men and women truly mattered. Gutta could never be confused with being a member of some black revolutionary movement or social activist, but he was just a Black man who had enough of seeing violence perpetrated against his people and wanted to strike back at the powers that be to give them a taste of their own medicine. This would be his small contribution to the plight of African Americans to receive fair and just treatment in this country.

When he hired John Lucci to investigate Balker's background, Gutta discovered that he was originally from Cheyenne, Wyoming and had ties to the Aryan Nations white supremacist organization which had its national headquarters in Hayden Lake, Idaho. He made regular contributions to the organization and attended their rallies in various parts of the country. Gutta also found out Balker had an older brother, Ryan, who was serving prison time for a vicious assault on a Black man who was married to a White woman. These factors made it clear to Gutta that Balker's actions were clearly racially motivated.

None of this information was brought to the light by the media throughout all of the coverage of Noel's death. The media did, however, attempt to paint Noel as being a thug when it was discovered in the autopsy toxicology reports he had a small amount of marijuana in his system. This just went to show the bias that existed in the media's coverage of any incident which had elements of racial injustice involved. It illustrated how easy it was for them to convey a negative image of young Black man to the world to attempt to justify him being the victim of a rogue and racist police officer.

Lucci was also able to locate Balker's current address. He lived in a rancher home in a quiet suburban neighborhood in Arlington, Virginia. He wasn't married and didn't have children, but lived alone with his Labrador retriever named Smokey. For this job, Gutta paid Jericho for this hit out of his own money. This was personal for him and he wanted the job carried out with precision. It had to be brutal to convey the clear message he desired to send: Black lives did matter and had just as much value as that of a White person. Jericho was clear about his assignment and was elated to carry it out to the letter. He felt Noel's mother's pain because he too experienced something similar when his mother died in that fire years ago as a result of the negligence of a money hungry, socially privileged White man who had no regard for a Black life.

As Jericho lurked in the background and hid behind a tree, he watched Balker enter his home alone. He had followed him all day long as he went about his daily routine. He waited for the sun to set before he made his move. Balker lived in a quiet neighborhood with minimal street activity because most of the residents were retirement aged individuals who were normally in the bed by eight o'clock in the evening. It was the perfect murder scene because there wouldn't be any witnesses and Jericho could handle his business and disappear into the night unobserved. Jericho cautiously ran across Balker's yard to get to the back of his property. He noticed Balker turn on the light in his kitchen and slowly crept up the stairs that led to his kitchen door. Before Balker could react, Jericho kicked in the door with his gun drawn. Balker's was totally caught off guard. He didn't have a chance to reach for the weapon he kept in the kitchen drawer.

"Please, don't shoot me. You can take whatever you want!" Balker pleaded while dropping to his knees in a submissive position. Jericho had to laugh at him because here he was this big bad racist cop when he was on the police force, but now he was on his knees like a punk pussy begging for his life. He almost couldn't believe this man was the same vicious killer who took young Noel's life. The irony was surreal.

"I don't want your money, old man. Get up off your knees, you coward. Let's go in the other room so we can have a little chat," Jericho uttered calmly with his gun still cocked. Balker got up and proceeded to walk toward his living room.

"Son, you don't want to do this. It would be a big mistake. I'm a retired police officer. If you do anything to me, the law won't look too kindly upon you being that you're Black, if you know what I mean," Balker attempted to reason with him. The racist pig Jericho thought he was had just surfaced. The funny thing about a bigot was he couldn't hide his true colors for too long before they started to show. To kill him would be a pleasure for Jericho. He would be one less devil who had a chance to take an innocent Black life.

"I know who you are, you racist bastard. You don't need to worry about what the law is going to do to me. You need to worry about what I'm about to do to you. Now, have a seat and shut your mouth!" Jericho ordered him. Balker did as he was told and sat down in his recliner chair.

"What are you talking about? How do you know me? I've never met you before in my life. I'm just a retired cop trying to live out my golden years in peace," he stated nervously. His fear caused him to urinate on himself. Jericho noticed the wetness form in the crotch area of his trousers. Balker tried to hide his discomfort and embarrassment with having to sit in his own piss, but it didn't work.

"All of you racist White boys are some punks. You're pissing in your pants now, but you didn't have any fear when you pulled the trigger and killed young Noel did you?" Jericho asked him directly. In an instant, Balker's entire demeanor and facial expression changed. He went from the image of the helpless old man he tried to sell to Jericho to the cocky bigot he truly was.

"His death was an accident. However, I don't feel guilty about ridding the Earth of another future Black criminal. He should've just kept his mouth shut and not ran when I approached him. He would be alive today," Balker declared as he chuckled.

He was proud of the fact he killed Noel. In his racist mind, Noel was one less nigga the world would have to incarcerate in the future with the tax dollars of hard working White American citizens. He felt like he did White America a favor by killing him. Jericho couldn't believe his arrogance when he attempted to shift the blame onto Noel for his own death. He was so enraged he walked over to him and slapped him across the face with his hand several times until his face was red. He took his gun and cracked him across the bridge of his nose. Blood gushed everywhere.

"Don't you ever call me, son, you racist pig. So, you're admitting that you killed Noel?" Jericho asked for clarification.

"Yeah, I killed the little bastard. I told him several times before that if I saw him and his friend on that corner again I was taking them to jail. He ran his mouth to me one too many times with his slick backtalk telling me he had a right to stand on that corner because he wasn't breaking the law. When I saw him that day and I approached him and his friend, he called me a punk cop and told me to get out of his face before he took off running. I chased him into the alley, we fought, and I shot him. I guess we see who the punk is now, huh?" he laughed as he wiped the blood from his face with his hand. He felt no need to deny the truth anymore given his current circumstances. Jericho stood before him with a gun in his hand and he was clearly there to take his life.

"Thank you for your confession, you idiot, I got just what I needed from you," Jericho stated before he pulled the trigger on his gun six times.

All of the bullets hit Balker in the face. His funeral would definitely be a closed casket service. The gunshots were muffled out by the silencer on Jericho's gun. Balker's neighbors didn't hear a thing when he viciously executed him. He spray painted the words "Stop Killing Young Black Men" in black paint in all capital letters across the living room wall. He ripped open Balker's shirt and carved Noel's full name on his chest with his knife. He reached inside of his bag and pulled out a picture of Noel that he downloaded offline. He placed it inside of Balker's hands and folded his arms across his chest. The picture was soaked in his blood. When his body was discovered, he wanted the world to know why Balker was killed so there was no confusion.

Originally, Jericho planned to torture Balker before he killed him to get a recorded confession like Gutta instructed him to do. However, when Balker voluntarily admitted to the killing, it made his job that much easier. Gutta intended to share the recording with the media, through an anonymous source, as evidence of the reality of police brutality in the black community. Jericho planned to edit the tape, of course, to remove any connection he had to Balker's murder. When he was done cleaning up the murder scene, he let out a loud sigh of relief and he hopped into his car. His soul was satisfied and his thirst for another victim to claim was fulfilled. He also hoped once Balker's death hit the news, Noel's mother could rest a little easier to know her son's death was avenged. This was one Black child whose death was not in vain. Jericho was proud of his work.

Chapter 8

"Hey, look who finally decided to wake up," Bunchy stated as he watched Elias begin to move about on the bed. He regained consciousness several times along the ride from his house to the warehouse where they held him captive. The bed was positioned in the middle of the floor of the empty, abandoned warehouse infamously called The Redrum room. The building was owned by the Caprese Foundation through a shell company. There were no signs of life in the surrounding area other than the mice and rats who roamed about the trash and debris which littered the streets. It was situated in the perfect location to torture someone or commit a murder without any witnesses around.

"Well, it's about time. For a minute, I thought I had killed the poor guy," Arturo joked.

"Nobody told you to hit him in the first place. You better be lucky you didn't kill him because you would have a whole other set of problems on your hands," Bunchy advised him.

While the two men went back and forth, Elias lifted his head off of the pillow and sat up on the bed. He rubbed his arms and wrists because they were sore from the rope that was tied around them. When he looked up to the ceiling, the room was spinning around. He did his best to regain his bearings, but he was still dazed from the blow to the head Arturo delivered. He had a massive headache. When he took his hand and rubbed his head, he could feel the crust from the dried up blood on his scalp in the area where he was hit. His vision was blurry. He tried to focus his eyes on the images of his two abductors who sat down on a large sofa across from him, but all he saw was a double image of both men. He felt groggy and discombobulated.

"What am I doing here? What do you want from me? Where am I?" Elias asked.

"You'll find out soon enough, old man. This will all be over with soon enough," Bunchy responded. He turned his attention back to the television in front of him. There was a long extension cord running from it that was plugged into a portable power generator a good distance away from where they were seated. He pointed the remote control in his hand at the television to change the channel.

He chose to watch a rerun episode of the hit television show *Power* on the Starz network.

"Can I at least get something to drink?" Elias asked. He observed the half empty bottle of alcohol seated next to Arturo's foot.

"You want a sip of this good stuff right here, huh?" Arturo teased him. He now held the pint of whisky in his hand and dangled it in front of Elias' face. He saw the eager look in his eyes and knew it well. Arturo was an alcoholic himself and knew the soothing feeling a stiff drink delivered to his soul on a nightly basis.

"Yes, please. I need it badly," Elias uttered without a hint of pride. He had no shame because he knew he was a helpless drunk. He wasn't even a whisky drinker, but he didn't care at the moment. He would drink rubbing alcohol if he could right now because that was how bad he wanted a drink.

"Here, drink the rest of this and keep quiet until we tell you to speak. You're interrupting my show," Arturo stated. He extended his arm out to give him the bottle of whisky. Elias took it in his hand and put the bottle to his lips. Within a few seconds, the bottle was empty. Elias closed his eyes and let the devil's nectar take its effect. The whisky warmed his insides and gave him a sense of comfort in the most uncomfortable of situations. Here he was a man being held hostage for an unknown reason, but he curled back up on the bed and drifted back off to sleep like a newborn baby who didn't have a care in the world.

"Man, this guy Ghost is a beast. He can get himself out of any situation," Bunchy stated in reference to the main character of the show. He was played by actor Omari Hardwick. The character he played was a drug kingpin who was struggling to get out of the street life.

"Yeah, he's a crafty guy, but Tommy doesn't mess around either. He's a killer," Arturo chimed in. Both men were clearly totally immersed in the drama and action of the show as though the characters being portrayed were real people.

"Does Ghost remind you of somebody that we know?" Bunchy asked.

They both looked at each other and laughed. The similarities between Ghost and their boss, Geno, were too evident not to notice. They both were highly intelligent gangsters who desired a better life outside of the streets. They both were just as vicious as they were diplomatic when it came to handling business in both the streets and the corporate world. They both always seemed to remain a step ahead of the law and the competition. The only difference between the two was that Ghost was a fictional character on the television screen and Geno was the real deal in the real world.

The two men went back and forth in conversation about the rest of the episode while they awaited further instructions about what to do with Elias. As the show was about to end, they heard a loud sound that startled them. The front doors of the warehouse opened up. Geno's Mercedes-Maybach slowly crept toward them and parked. Clay hopped out of the driver's seat to open the door for Geno. When Geno walked toward them, Bunchy clicked off the television. Both Arturo and Bunchy's demeanor shifted from a laid back mood to a more serious one. Geno's mere presence commanded that level of respect from his workers whenever he entered the room.

"Hello, gentleman, I hope you have been hospitable to our guest. I trust he has received the best care possible given the unfortunate circumstances," Geno inquired.

"Absolutely, Geno, we've taken good care of Mr. Knox," Bunchy chimed in.

"He gave us a little bit of a struggle at first, but he has since settled down, isn't that right?" Arturo asked as he glanced in Elias's direction. He was awakened out of his sleep by the sound of Geno's car when it entered the garage. Elias simply nodded his head in agreement while he rubbed his eyes. Given the circumstances, it was the smartest response for him to have. When he looked at Geno, he recognized his face.

"Hey, I know who you are. You're that big time attorney I see on television and on those billboards all over the city. You're Geno Caprese," Elias uttered. He mustered up the strength to sit up. Now he was really clueless. He wondered to himself what in the world a powerful man like Geno would want with him. After all, he was just a drunk, retired postal worker. He couldn't figure out why in the world he would even be on his radar for any reason.

"Yes, that's me. It's nice to meet you, Mr. Knox. I'm sorry we couldn't have met under better circumstances," Geno stated. He walked over to where he was seated and shook his hand.

"What in the world am I doing here? What could a man like you want from me?" Elias asked.

"I'm glad you asked me that question. It's very simple. It has been brought to my attention that you told the police that you saw the people who killed your neighbor, Marcus Harrison, is that correct?" Geno inquired.

Police Commissioner Leftwich recently contacted Geno and gave him Elias' name and address as he requested. The cop in him hated giving up the identity of a witness in a case, but he had no choice. If he didn't do what Geno wanted him to do, Geno would surely ruin his life if he exposed his secret to the world. He would lose his job. His family would be devastated. He would go to jail for being a pedophile. As much as he hated giving the information to Geno, his survival instinct kicked in. It was either Elias or himself and he chose to save his own neck.

It all started to make sense to Elias. The picture became clear. He now understood how he wound up in his current position. This all had to do with the statement he made to the police about Marcus' murder. He told the police he wouldn't testify in court about what he saw once they apprehended the suspects, but they threatened to arrest him if he didn't comply. It had been a minute since the murder occurred and since he heard anything else from the police. He just assumed that Marcus' death would just be another unsolved murder of a Black man in Baltimore City. Given his current predicament, that clearly was not the case.

"I told the police what the guy and the two girls looked like, but also said I'm not testifying in court to anything. They threatened to lock me up if I didn't come in to the police department and make a statement. I'm an old lonely man. I just want to live out my final years in peace. I don't want any problems with anybody," Elias pleaded. He glanced at his captors and Geno. He sensed they were dangerous men and his life hung in the balance.

"Relax, Mr. Knox, we mean you no harm unless you chose not to cooperate. I'm glad to hear that you don't want to testify in court. That is exactly the response I wanted to hear from you. It's in your best interest as well in the best of interest of an associate of mine you forget what you saw that night," Geno suggested. However, the menacing look on his face implied his statement was more than just a suggestion. It was a direct threat. How Elias responded to the threat would determine his fate.

"Mr. Caprese, you don't have to worry about me saying a thing. I can promise you that, Sir. Please, don't hurt me! Please don't hurt me!" he begged.

"Breathe easy, my friend. Everything is going to be alright. Today is your lucky day. I'm going to give you a new lease on life. What would you say if I gave you fifty thousand dollars in cash to forget about what you saw and to leave Baltimore for good?" Geno asked.

"I would take it in a heartbeat, Sir. You won't have to worry about seeing me in this city ever again. I can promise you that for sure!" Elias stated enthusiastically. When he added the money up in his head, the thought of what he could do with it made him forgot all about the pain he felt from the blow to the head he took.

"Well, then we have ourselves a deal, Mr. Knox. However, I want to advise you that if you break our deal, I can't promise you that nothing will happen to you or your son and his family. They live in Virginia and he's a chiropractor, is that correct?" Geno uttered to drive home his point.

"We are on the same page, Mr. Caprese. You won't ever hear from me again," Elias replied.

"Okay, well then it's settled. My men will keep you company here until we complete our business. I'm glad we could reach an understanding. Enjoy the rest of your life," Geno said rather calmly.

Geno shook Elias' hand as a show of good faith before he hopped back in his car. He planned to make arrangements for Elias to receive the payment for the amount agreed upon shortly. Once the transaction was completed, Elias would be free to live his life as he chose so as long as he held up his end of the bargain. He was well aware of the consequences of going back on his word to a man like Geno. As things stood, the police department no longer had an eyewitness to Marcus' murder who could identify Jericho, Shavon, or Nina. That alone would be a major blow to any effort they made to try and prosecute them for the crime. With Elias soon to be out of the picture, he just needed Jarvis to make good on his promise and he could put this issue to bed.

Chapter 9

Marietta Caprese sat by her husband's bedside and thought about the wonderful life they shared together for so many years. She held his hand in her hands and rubbed it ever so gently. Marietta found herself overcome with emotions to have to view her precious Leonardo in such a feeble state. She wished she could just snap her fingers and he would be cancer-free, but she knew that wasn't going to happen. At this point, the only thing that could save Leonardo was divine intervention. Although she prayed daily for a miracle, she accepted the inevitable and resolved herself to cherishing whatever time they had left together.

She reminisced about the first time they met and how Leonardo gracefully swept her off her feet. She remembered like it was yesterday the expression on his face when he got down on one knee and asked for her hand in marriage. It was a day she would never forget because it changed the course of her entire life. Once she agreed to marry Leonardo, she took a lifetime oath to be his exclusively. She stood by that vow for their entire marriage. No other man could even get as much as a second look from her. Marietta loved her Leonardo with every ounce of her heart and soul.

She was proud of how their union of love produced three handsome sons. However, despite all of the sacrifices she made for her Leonardo and her children, he didn't give her the same level of commitment. When she found out about his relationship with Jericho's mother, she was crushed. To know he actually fell in love with Raylene filled her with a level hurt which she could forgive, but never forget. The hurt still stung after all of these years. As she stared at him, a part of her wanted to unplug all of the machines he was hooked up to and end his life, but it would go against her peaceful spirit to do such a thing. Plus, she loved him too much to do him harm. For better or worse, she was stuck with Leonardo Caprese.

"Marietta, where are my sons? Where's Silvio? Where's Geno? Where's Cesare? I want to see my boys!" he demanded. He tried to get up out of the bed, but his frail frame became wrapped up in all of the tubes that were inserted into his body.

"Calm down, my love. They will be here soon. Don't get yourself all worked up. You need to conserve your strength," she tried to advise him, but Leonardo wouldn't listen.

He pushed the button in his hand to release another shot of morphine from the IV bag that hung from the pole next to his bed. He was pissed when he realized he had already used it all. He banged his frail hand on the rail of the bed and winced from the pain. He was frustrated and evil as could be. He didn't feel as though he deserved to suffer with cancer, but all of the cigarettes he smoked and alcohol he drank made him a prime candidate for the disease.

"I need to make things right with Geno. He hates me but I need to make him understand that I know I messed up and I'm sorry!" he yelled.

"He knows you love him, Leo. He knows it deep down inside his heart. He'll come around. I need you to rest, my love," she pleaded.

Marietta knew Geno had no intention of stopping by the hospice facility to see his father. Since he told him about Jericho and Shavon, Geno had not been back to their home or called to check on them. However, Carina did bring the children to see their grandfather several times. Geno didn't object because if he did, he would have to explain the entire situation to them and he wasn't ready to do so just yet. He needed to sort things out for himself first.

Marietta missed her favorite son dearly. He had never gone so long without being in contact with her no matter how busy he was with work or other things. However, she knew he was just as stubborn as his father was. He got the trait honestly. As for Silvio, the last thing Geno told her about him was that he got himself into trouble with the law and was on the run. Her motherly instinct told her something bad happened or was about to happen to him. She didn't tell this news to Leonardo because he would be upset and concerned, which was the last thing he needed given his current physical state. Marietta would be devastated to know he was really dead and that Geno had him killed. Cesare came by a few times to see Leonardo out of respect because he was still his father, but there was still an emotional disconnect between them due to their long standing strained relationship. While she sat on the edge of the bed and tried to calm Leonardo down, the doctor entered the room,

"How are you today, Mrs. Caprese? How is your husband doing today? What seems to be the problem?" Dr. Nolan Stevens asked.

"Why don't you ask me how I'm doing since I'm right here? You don't have to talk about me like I'm dead and can't speak for myself. What kind of man are you?" Leonardo asked in an irritated state.

"I'm sorry, Mr. Caprese. I didn't mean to offend you. How are you feeling today, sir?"

"I feel like shit. I want to get out of here now!" Leonardo demanded angrily.

"Leo, he didn't mean you any harm. He's just doing his job. Calm yourself down," she barked at him. Marietta was at her wits end dealing with his erratic mood swings.

"If you calm down, Mr. Caprese, I'll have the nurse bring you more medication to ease the pain. How does that sound?" Dr. Stevens attempted to bargain with him.

"Now that's more like it, Doc. Can a fella get a drink and a smoke around this place? Hell, I'm dying anyway so it sure as hell can't hurt me any further," Leonardo rationalized.

"We'll see what we can do about that later on, Sir," Dr. Stevens replied calmly.

He had no intention of granting his wishes. He made the statement to appease him and to get Leonardo to calm down. Minutes later, the nurse entered the room and installed a new morphine IV bag. Leonardo pressed the button several times to release the drug into his bloodstream. Once it began to take effect, Leonardo returned to a much more sedated state.

"I just want to see my sons, Marietta. I have to make them understand how much I love them. I want to see Jericho and Shavon too. I hope they don't hate me for being such a bad father. I love them all," he rambled on in a childlike voice.

"I will do my best, my love. I will do my best," she promised him.

Shortly thereafter, he drifted off to sleep. It hurt to hear him mention Jericho and Shavon in the same breath as her children, but she had to acknowledge they were his offspring as well. She had no clue how to get in contact with them, but she knew if anybody could find them Geno could. She had to find a way to grant him his one wish to see all of his children before he passed away. She understood Geno's initial angry reaction when he found out about his other siblings, but in spite of his disappointment, Leonardo was still his father. He was still the same man who raised him. He wasn't perfect, but he was a good man. As his wife, if she could forgive him for his flaws as a husband, then she saw no reason why Geno couldn't do the same. For better or worse, they were all still family. If she wanted to get Geno to come see his father before he died, she knew there was only person who could make Geno put his hurt and anger aside to fulfill a dying man's last wish and that was Carina. She planned to give her a call once she returned home because she didn't know how much longer Leonardo had to live.

Chapter 10

Geno was on the tail end of another long day at work. He had just finished meeting with three new potential clients whom he planned to assign to several of his junior associates at the law firm. While he sat at his desk, he reviewed the final terms of the plea deal he negotiated for Lincoln Bukowski. As he looked over the document, he smiled in admiration of his own craftiness in being able to negotiate terms for his client he knew no other lawyer in town could deliver. After weeks of grueling cross examinations, legal maneuvering, and various motions being filed by both sides, the prosecution realized that a guilty verdict against Lincoln would be a difficult task to achieve. It was almost a crap shoot because both sides made compelling arguments for the jury to ponder. Consequently, at the last minute, the State decided to settle for a plea deal as opposed to walking away empty handed with no conviction at all.

Under the terms of the deal Geno negotiated, Lincoln would plead guilty to sexual assault in the third degree, a crime punishable by a maximum sentence of ten years in jail. Geno was able to convince the State's Attorney to offer Lincoln a three years jail sentence, with eighteen months of the sentence suspended. While he was incarcerated as well as when he was released, Lincoln would have to undergo drug treatment to deal with his drug addiction.

To plead Lincoln's case, Geno argued that Lincoln wasn't a bad person, but it was his drug use that was the root cause of his deviant behavior. He also used Judge Bukowski's social status as an upstanding member of the Baltimore community as leverage to make the deal more saleable. Initially, Lincoln wasn't happy he had to go to prison, but when he realized the case could go either way and he could receive a much longer sentence if he were convicted, he reluctantly accepted the deal.

Judge Bukowski was relieved the case was finally over so the media could move on to more important topics other than what he called his family's "personal issues". He was grateful for the brilliant legal work Geno did on his son's behalf. This case was another victory in court for Geno to add to his extensive resume. All he had to wait for now was Lincoln's court date so the plea deal could be made official.

In addition to his success in the courtroom, he had also just wrapped up a major international distribution deal for CITD with GameWorld Distributors which would significantly increase the company's revenue stream over the next few years by allowing for them to reach a far wider customer base. He was negotiating with his fellow board member, Giovanni Giordano, the terms of them doing a joint venture together in developing a clothing line which would be an extension of the Giordano Fashions brand. Whereas Giovanni's clothing line appealed to an exclusive upscale clientele, the new clothing line would cater to the urban market greatly influenced by the hip hop culture.

Geno was sold on the idea of entering the fashion industry after he reviewed all of the detailed research Cesare had done. He saw the money making potential in the endeavor and decided to dive in head first with bringing it into fruition. Giovanni initially was against the idea because he thought it would tarnish his image with his customer base who were used to his expensive high end designs, but he warmed up to the idea after Geno agreed to assume all of the financial risk for the venture and still make him a partner with a forty percent stake in the deal. He had access to all of the important connections in the fashion industry while Geno had the money to put behind the idea to make it a success.

If his life were a game a poker, then it was safe to say Geno was dealt a royal flush. He had more than the Midas touch because everything he touched turned out to be a platinum success. He had already made enough money to live like a King for the rest of his life, but it wasn't enough. No matter what level of success he achieved, Geno still craved more. He thrived off of his ability to outthink his opponents and competition. He genuinely believed no one was smarter than him. Some would say he was arrogant, but he strongly disagreed with that assessment of his character.

It was his belief that when someone exuded a high level of self-confidence in their abilities, it's not arrogance if they could deliver favorable results repeatedly to validate their assertions. Every business decision he made was well thought out and strategically planned. He left little room for error in his dealings in both the business arena and the courtroom. Simply put, Geno was as good as advertised at everything he set out to do in life. It made some people mad to see him win so much, but he could care less. He considered himself to be blessed by the Creator and entitled to live a life fit for a King.

"Excuse me, Geno; your wife is on the phone. She's on line one. Do you want me to put her through?" Jia asked over the phone intercom system.

"Yes, you can put her through," he replied. A few seconds later, his phone beeped and he picked up the receiver.

"Hey, honey, are you busy?" Carina asked.

"I'm never too busy for my favorite girl. I'm just wrapping up things here in the office and I was about to head home," he replied.

"I was just wondering since I'm not too far from Maggie's right now, I was thinking we could meet there and have dinner," she suggested.

"What about the kids?" he asked.

"They're both home. I got us a babysitter for the night because I wanted to spend some quality time with my wonderful husband for a few hours," she replied.

"That sounds good to me. Give me about ten minutes to wrap up things here and I'll meet you there within the hour," he stated.

"Okay, honey, I'll see you there," Carina stated before she hung up the phone.

Geno filed away his copy of Lincoln's plea deal in a manila folder he left in the center of his desk. He waited for his computer to shut down before he exited his office. He gave Jia some last minute instructions for several letters he needed typed and mailed out in the morning. After he had everything wrapped up at the office, he made his way to the elevator flanked by his security detail. When he stepped off the elevator, he called Clay to have him bring his car to the front of the building. Within fifteen minutes, he arrived and Geno hopped in the back seat. Clay sped off en route to Maggie's. Geno's bodyguards followed closely behind them in a separate car.

"How was your day, Geno?" Clay asked.

"My day was phenomenal, Clay. Hell, every day for me is phenomenal. I can't complain about one thing in my life right now. I have two awesome kids and I'm on my way to meet my beautiful wife for dinner. Yeah, everything is good for me," Geno replied.

"That's good to hear, Geno. You're a lucky man," Clay stated.

"There's nothing lucky about my success, Clay. It's all about skillful planning and having the balls to go out and take what you want out of life. You can't wait around for opportunity to come to you. You've got to go out and make it happen for yourself," Geno advised him. He loved to impart jewels of wisdom about success onto Clay every time he escorted him around town.

"I'm taking notes, Geno. I'm taking notes," Clay responded.

"That's what I like to hear. Now turn the radio to the *Watercolors* station so I can mellow out to some smooth jazz until we reach the restaurant," Geno instructed him.

Geno reclined back in his seat and closed his eyes. His mind got lost in the music. After about twenty minutes of driving in downtown traffic, they arrived at their destination. Clay parked the car in Geno's reserved parking spot in front of the restaurant and hopped out to open his door. Geno made his way inside of the restaurant to his table in the private section in the rear area. Carina was already seated at the table. They had the section to themselves.

"There's my beautiful wife," Geno stated proudly. Carina could do nothing but blush. Geno kissed her on the cheek gently and seated himself across from her.

"I took the liberty of ordering us a bottle of red wine and the fried tortellini for an appetizer," she stated.

"That sounds tasty. So, how was your day, love?" he asked.

"I didn't do anything spectacular. I just went shopping and stopped by your mother's house to spend some time with her. She's holding up pretty good considering the circumstances," she replied referencing his father's steadily declining health. She took a sip from her glass of wine.

"That's good to hear she's doing fine. I need to give her a call," he replied rather nonchalantly.

While he sipped on his glass of wine, their conversation was interrupted when the waiter returned to the table to take their dinner orders. Once they were done ordering, Carina picked up where she left off in their conversation.

"We also went to see your father. He's not doing too well, Geno. He asked to see you several times," Carina stated.

Carina knew him and his father had a falling out, but he never told her exactly why. She knew him well enough to know not to press Geno for information. He was the kind of man that when he was ready to talk about something, he would do so in his own time and on his own terms. However, given his father's terminal condition, time was of the essence. She refused to let Geno's stubborn nature deprive him of spending time with his father during his last days. She had to give it her best shot to convince him to change his mind.

"Let's not talk about him, Carina. Let's enjoy our evening together," Geno stated. He found himself beginning to get agitated at the mention of Leonardo's name.

"Geno, your mother told me everything and I understand why you're upset with your father. You feel betrayed because he had two children out of wedlock. You have a right to feel that way, baby, but that's his sin he has to answer for one day. He made a mistake, but he's still your father, baby."

Please go see him before he passes away. You don't want to him to die without you two making amends. That's a big burden to carry around for the rest of your life," she tried to reason with him.

"Carina, you're my wife and I love you dearly, but you need to mind your business," he urged her.

"Geno, don't ever talk to me like that again. I'm your wife and the mother of your children. You will talk to me with respect," she demanded. She was submissive to him as her husband, but Carina also knew when to be firm and stand her ground. It was one of the many attributes she had which made Geno fall in love with her.

"I apologize for my tone, but some things are better left alone. This is one of those situations. My mother had no right telling you about that situation at all. She was totally out of line. Carina, please drop the subject so we can enjoy this good meal," he pleaded with her. While they went back and forth, the waiter brought out their main entrees.

"Geno, I know you better than anybody on this Earth other than your mother. I know that despite all of the anger you have with your father, you also still love him. Put your feelings aside and be the bigger man in this situation. I'm asking you, as your wife, to make peace with your father," she stated even more emphatically.

"I'm done talking about this subject. You can have this conversation with yourself. I'm going to enjoy this good food," Geno stated. He proceeded to dig into the plate of lasagna that was in front of him.

"Geno, I love you dearly, but you can be an asshole sometimes. You can enjoy your food alone. I'm going home. You can sleep in one of the guest rooms tonight," Carina stated angrily. She got up from the table and stormed off. Geno knew she was right, but his pride wouldn't let him admit it to her. He wanted to go see his father, but his ego stood in the way. He also knew Carina was just as stubborn and wouldn't let the situation go until he did the right thing. After the disrespectful way he just talked to Carina, he had some serious making up to do to get back in her good graces. His great day just turned to shit that quickly.

Chapter 11

Cesare's office at the Caprese Foundation's headquarters was in no way, shape, or form what one would expect to see an executive have inside of a multi-million dollar corporation. There was no expensive furniture or ritzy paintings on the walls. He didn't have a plush leather chair to sit in while he reclined back with his feet up on his desk. There was no fancy bookshelf filled with a host of relevant book titles for him to use as a reference guide in his daily professional activities. Instead, his office space included a comfortable black sofa made of a soft microfiber material that was positioned directly in front of a seventy inch 4k Ultra HD television which was professionally mounted on the wall. Connected to the television were his Playstation 4, Microsoft Xbox One, and Nintendo Wii gaming consoles. He had a state of the art surround sound stereo system installed to enhance the sound experience of the video games he was responsible for testing out before they hit the retail market.

There were various game controllers scattered all over the floor. He had a mini-refrigerator filled with different types of soft drinks and snacks within arm's reach of the sofa. He had posters of different video games posted all over the walls. He kept the lights dim inside of the office because it was conducive to creating a more pleasurable gaming experience for him. His office resembled a teenager's game room in the basement of his parent's home more so than the office of the Vice-President of a rapidly growing and soon to be a Fortune 500 company. When he hired him, Geno gave him the freedom to furnish it as he saw fit. He told him to make his work environment as comfortable as possible for him and that was exactly what Cesare did.

Thus far, Cesare's life transition from an aspiring rapper to a working member of corporate America had been a relatively smooth one. This was largely due to the fact his older brother happened to be the CEO of the corporation. There was no lengthy interview process conducted. He didn't to have to go through an extensive training program when he began working at the company. Not only did Geno see to it he was made a member of the Caprese Foundation board of directors, he was also appointed as the Vice-President of

Caprese Innovative Technology Designs, or CITD, the acronym the company was more popularly known by in the video gaming world. He started out with a healthy six figure salary which suited him just fine. He drove a brand new royal blue BMW 750Li, which was leased by the Foundation. He even moved out of Geno's house into his own two bedroom condominium in the luxurious Ritz-Carlton Residences located right near the pricy Inner Harbor area. The oversized walk-in closet inside of his condo was filled with just as many tailor made suits as jeans and Polo shirts. In a short span of time, Cesare adjusted to his new role of being a businessman and got more comfortable in the role with each passing day.

As for school, Geno permitted him to adjust his work schedule so he could attend some classes in the daytime and others in the evening. Now that he was drug-free, Cesare was able to put his maximum effort into his coursework. Thus far, he had maintained a straight A average in his classes. Cesare set himself on a course to be able to complete his Bachelor's degree in three years instead of four. Working at the Foundation, he got a taste of the good life and there was no turning back for him. Rap music was no longer a top priority in his life other than when he was riding his car or relaxing in his condo. His full focus and attention now was on climbing up the corporate ladder. Geno gave him the opportunity of a lifetime and he planned to give it his all to take full advantage.

Cesare and his new boss at CITD, Jeremy Wisby, got along well and had a great relationship. Initially, there was some awkwardness between them because Jeremy sensed that Geno placed Cesare in his position with the sole purpose of totally taking over his company. However, after the two had a chance to get to know each other, Jeremy realized that wasn't the case. In fact, he found Cesare's input into the design process to be very useful. The best experts to give feedback on how good a video game were the actual gamers who spent hours each day in front of the television with a controller in their hands playing them. He was genuinely impressed with the wealth of knowledge Cesare possessed about the current trends in the gaming industry. Cesare read every gaming magazine on the market and stayed in all of the trendiest online gaming blogs to stay updated on all of the upcoming games the competition had on the horizon.

To have a business partner who was just as up to speed with this kind of information as he was proved to be useful to Jeremy. By delegating some of his duties and responsibilities to Cesare, he could now dedicate more of his time to the design aspect of the gaming business so CITD could stay on the cusp of groundbreaking gaming innovations. They oversaw a staff of fifteen employees and college interns who helped them to keep the company afloat. If the two of them stayed on the same page and followed Geno's leadership, CITD could be a major player in the gaming industry for years to come.

"Hey, Cesare, what's happening dude?" Jeremy asked as he burst into his office without knocking. Cesare was busy engaged in an intense gaming session.

Jeremy looked like your stereotypical image of a nerd or computer geek. He was tall and lanky with jet black, frizzy hair that always looked unkempt. He wore a pair of thick, geeky looking horn rimmed glasses with super thick lenses because he was blind as a bat. He dressed in cheap wrinkled, no named clothing he bought from the thrift store. He always wore a pair of canvas Converse sneakers that looked worse for the wear. He said the shoes were a good luck charm because he wore them the whole time he was in the process of developing the first video game that launched the company. He talked in a slow, methodical manner making sure he pronounced all of his words clearly. He didn't have a girlfriend because he was married to his work. When he wasn't at the office, he spent most of his time at home alone.

"Man, this Beast Stalker game is something serious. I've already made it up to the third level. I think we have another winner on our hands with this one. I love the response time for the weapons on this game," Cesare replied enthusiastically about the demo version of the newest gaming software Jeremy designed.

"I'm glad you like it. I hope the consumers feel the same way," Jeremy replied. He took all praise about his work in stride because he was humble.

"You don't have to worry about that at all. All of these teenagers who want a game with a lot of violence and action scenes will be breaking their necks to have their parents buy this for the holidays. The 3D graphics are amazing and detailed. The characters look like they want to jump off the screen!" Cesare continued in his praise of the new game. The plan was to have it ready for release during the upcoming Thanksgiving holiday season which was still a few months away. They wanted to take advantage of all of the people who would be doing their early Christmas shopping during the Black Friday weekend.

"That's cool, dude. Have you had a chance to review the marketing plan I laid out?" Jeremy asked.

"Yeah, I've glanced at it. Everything looks good. I think you did a good analysis of the target audience. Man enough of all of this business talk. How about we go out to a club this weekend so we can scope out some chicks and have a good time?" Cesare offered.

"I don't know about that because I have a lot of work to do," Jeremy replied. He had absolutely no social life at all. If he wasn't work in his office, then he was at home working.

"You need to forget about the office sometimes, Jeremy. You could use a break. Besides, keep it real with me, when was the last time you got laid?" Cesare asked him bluntly.

Jeremy couldn't even respond to the question. The look on his face said it all. He couldn't recall the last time he was with a woman. Growing up, he had a hard time getting dates in high school and college because all of the girls saw him as a nerd. He only had one girlfriend his entire life and they broke up when he moved to Baltimore after he sold the company to Geno. He was definitely in need of some female companionship.

"Cesare, you are absolutely right; I do need to get out more. Where do you want to go?" Jeremy asked.

"I know a few spots in Georgetown that we can check out. However, before we do anything, dude you need a makeover. We need to get you some new clothes. After all, you're a millionaire now. It's time that you looked the part. Don't worry about a thing because after I'm done with you, the ladies will be all over you," Cesare promised him.

"I'm game to party. Let's make it happen, dude," Jeremy stated in an attempt to sound hip.

He couldn't argue with the truth Cesare just spoke about him. He needed an image makeover if he wanted to finally come out of his shell and have an active social life.

"Cool. I'll set everything up," Cesare stated.

As they conversed, they were interrupted by a knock at Cesare's office door. Seconds later, Geno stepped inside of his office. His presence was a surprise because he rarely came down to their floor in the building. Geno gave Jeremy a free reign to run the company as he saw fit because video gaming was his area of expertise. Geno just handled the contractual and distribution aspects of the business. Plus, with Cesare now working with him, he had a set of eyes and ears involved in the daily operations of the company he knew he could trust. That meant his investment would be well protected.

"Hey, fellas, how are things going? You two seem to be having too much fun down here. I hope some work is getting done," Geno teased them.

"Geno, you've got to try this new game out Jeremy designed. You will love it. When you see the sales figures once this hits the streets I think you will be very pleased," Cesare interjected.

"Now that's what I like to hear. In fact, that's part of my reason for coming down here. I need you two to come take a ride with me. I have a meeting lined up today with a new wholesale distributor and I want you guys to tag along. We can conduct some business, eat some good food, and you can tell me all about this new game you have in the works," Geno stated.

When he looked at Cesare, Geno's face beamed with pride. He was happy to see him so enthusiastic and personally involved with his work. It gave him a sense of purpose and he seemed to be highly motivated to do his best at his job. He was happy to see him make manifest all of the potential he always knew he had inside of him. His vision of having him by his side as he built the Caprese dynasty had started to come full circle. Unlike Silvio, he could count on Cesare to remain loyal to the family.

"That works for me. I'm starving. Hey Geno, I've finally talked Jeremy into hanging out with me this weekend. We're going to hit the clubs and he's going to let me hook him up with a new wardrobe. I'ma have to show him how the Caprese men get down with the ladies," Cesare bragged.

"Is that right? Well, Jeremy, don't let Cesare get you into trouble out in the streets chasing those women all hours of the night. I need you to stay on your A game so we can keep building on all of the success we've had thus far," Geno advised him.

Truth be told, he was glad to see Cesare and Jeremy developing such a good relationship. He too had noticed Jeremy's less than stellar wardrobe, but didn't say a thing because adding Jeremy's company to the Caprese business portfolio was one of his wisest business moves thus far. If he wanted to dress in second hand clothes, it was fine with him as long as the money kept rolling in.

"Don't worry, Geno, I can hold my own," Jeremy tried to reassure him.

"Yeah, Geno, he will be just fine," Cesare chimed to cosign Jeremy.

"Fellas, let's get outta here. I'll have Clay bring the car around to take us to the restaurant," Geno stated.

"Hey, Geno, before we leave out, let me bend your ear about something in private," Cesare interjected. Jeremy took his statement as cue for him to exit. He walked back down to his office to wait for them.

"What's on your mind? Is everything okay?" Geno asked.

"Yeah, I'm good, but it's Mom who's not doing too well. She's missing you. When I went to the hospital the other day to see Pops I could see it in her face. You know you always were her favorite. Even though Leo and I have never got along, he's still my father. He looks bad, man. You need to go see him," Cesare stated.

"You sound just like my wife. You need to remember who is the big brother in our relationship and who's the little brother. I give you guidance and not the other way around," Geno scolded him. He shot Cesare a look to suggest he had stepped out of his lane.

"You don't have to talk to me like that, Geno. Show me the same respect I show you. I'm just as much of a man as you are. I was just making a suggestion, but you can do what you want to do," Cesare shot back. He used to always back down when Geno berated him, but those days were over. He was a new man and not afraid to stand his ground.

"You're right, lil' bro. I apologize because I was out of line to talk you like that. This whole ordeal has been hard on me. Leo let me down in a major way. I thought we had a tight relationship, but for him to keep a secret like that from me all of these, I see now that's not the case. I hear what you're saying, lil' bro. I promise you I'll give Mom a call. Give me some time to really think about this entire situation. For now, let's go get something to eat while we take care of some business," Geno stated in an attempt to change the subject.

Truthful, not speaking to his mother had weighed heavily on his mind the past few days. He planned to give her a call. As for his father, that was another story. He needed more time to get over his anger at him. At the moment, he didn't have time to deal with personal stuff. He was in CEO mode. Making money was on his mind. He pulled out his cell phone to call Clay. Shortly thereafter, Clay pulled up in the front of the building and they were on their way to the lunch meeting Geno had set up. They were all excited about the potential for bigger things to come for the company. With Jeremy and Cesare working together to create the best gaming products possible and Geno handling all of the necessary negotiating with the distributors, CITD had a very bright future to look forward to in the business world.

Chapter 12

Homicide detective Elvin Swift was never happier to have pulled up to a red light because he didn't have the energy to drive any further. The sun was out when he started his work day, but the daylight gave way to the darkness of the night time by the time he was done. He was on the tail end of another double shift and was physically and mentally exhausted. His eyes were bloodshot red from being up for such a long period of time. It took all of the mental resolve he had inside to fight off the desire to fall asleep. He had almost nodded off several times along his journey back to the police station. He needed something to give him a boost of energy to help him stay awake which was why he decided to stop at Starbucks and get a cup of coffee a few minutes earlier.

Swift reached over to the cup holder in the center console to grab his cup of black coffee and took a sip. When he tasted it, he realized it was missing something. He grabbed the three packets of sugar on his passenger seat, ripped them open, and poured them into his cup. He stirred it with a spoon and once he was sure it was blended properly, he put the cup to his lips. He closed his eyes for a brief moment to savor the flavor. The caffeine rush, chased by the sugar, was just what he needed at the moment to perk him up. The time it took for the light to turn green seemed like an eternity. When it did, he pressed down on the pedal with his foot and accelerated. He sped off on his way back to the precinct. He decided to throw on his flashing lights so he could race through any red lights he encountered.

The last few months had been extremely busy for Swift and the Homicide division with the rash of tragic shootings that had occurred across the city. It seemed like every day he was called in to help investigate at least two new murder cases. Most of the murders were either a result of a drug beef, a gang related turf war, or the result of a domestic dispute. He had just left the scene of a double homicide of two young Black men.

According to the information he received, the two men were involved in a dispute over a dice game with another unidentified young Black male. It appeared as though the third man got upset because he lost money in the game and he became involved in a verbal dispute with several of the other men engaged in the dice game. Their argument escalated to the point that, out of nowhere, he pulled a gun from his waistband and opened fire on the entire group of individuals who were gambling. Several of the bullets struck the two victims. They both bled out and died on the scene as a result of their injuries. In the midst of the commotion, the shooter escaped on foot.

When he arrived to the location of the shooting, Detective Swift was given the task of interviewing witnesses to try and get a statement or some useful identifying information which could help the police arrest the shooter. However, as could be expected, none of the other men involved with the dice game or any of the neighborhood residents could identify the shooter because anyone who did provide information to the police would be labeled as a snitch. That was the worst title to have in the hood because snitching was a cardinal sin on the streets. With no witnesses to identify the suspect, Swift knew he had his work cut out for him to try and make an arrest.

If he had his way, he would just file this case right along with the other unsolved murder cases he had, but he knew it wouldn't be a wise choice on his part if he wanted to keep his job. With the heavy amount of media attention given to the recent rash of violent crimes in the city, there was a great deal of pressure on the homicide detectives coming from the upper leadership of the police department to solve a good number of the open murder cases. Next year was an election year and the Mayor wanted results to use as leverage in his re-election campaign. He needed statistical data to document his efforts to combat crime in the city and to make the streets appear to be safer for all of the residents of Baltimore. Consequently, he told Commissioner Leftwich what needed to be done. He told him that either the murder rate in the city went down or heads would roll. In other words, he would be unemployed if he didn't deliver results for the Mayor.

Commissioner Leftwich instructed all of his lieutenants, captains, and majors to convey to the police officers and detectives on the force that he needed arrests to be made soon or many of them would be out of a job right along with him. The message resonated loud and clearly with Swift. Being a police officer was his lifelong dream and he didn't plan on giving it up anytime soon. He was dedicated to the job and planned to deliver the results his superiors requested because he had his own aspirations to move up the food chain in the police department.

Swift pulled into the parking lot of the precinct and parked his car in an empty space. He got out and walked over to the building to finally clock out for the day. He couldn't wait to get to his bed to get some shuteye. He was hungry, but food could wait until he got some rest. He entered the building and didn't make it ten feet inside before his plans were interrupted when he heard his name called by Detective Putnam. He despised Putnam with a passion because he viewed him as a lazy cop with poor investigative skills. Swift and other officers used to joke about him all of the time. They said he was such a sorry cop that he couldn't close a case even if he had actual video footage because he would find some kind of way to mess it up. Swift's eyes rolled into the back of his head and he cursed under his breath to vent his frustration as he turned around to face Putnam.

"Swift, you've got someone waiting to see you. There's this guy who came in to confess to a murder, but that's not all. He even came in with the gun he killed the guy with and surrendered it voluntarily. How crazy is that? Man, I swear you get all of the easy cases. You're one lucky guy," Putnam stated enviously.

Swift was taken back when he stated the guy came into the police station to not only turn himself in, but that he also turned in the murder weapon. He had to make sure he heard Putnam correctly because it sounded too good to be true.

"So you're telling me he brought a gun in here? You have to be making this up, aren't you?" Swift inquired further.

"I wish I was making it up. He turned it in without the slightest bit of resistance. The guy's a junkie. He's as high as can be. You can go see for yourself," Putnam stated to confirm his earlier statement.

"So, why didn't you get up off your lazy butt and take his statement if the case is that easy? Why did you have to wait for me to get here?" he asked with a puzzled look on his face.

When he gave him a glance over, he noticed the donut in his hand and the jelly stain on his shirt. Putnam was a short, pudgy guy with a scraggly beard. His belly hung over his trousers. His cheeks were so fat they looked like they would explode at any moment. He smelled like somebody who walked around and passed gas all day long because he ate so much bad food. Swift couldn't even imagine him ever chasing a suspect without him falling out flat on his face or having a heart attack because he was so out of shape. He wondered to himself how Putnam ever passed the physical examination to even become a cop.

"Hey, I would have loved to have taken his statement, but he says he would only talk to you," Putnam replied.

"Whatever, man. Where is he?" Swift asked.

"He's in interrogation room no. 2," Putnam replied.

Reluctantly, Swift dragged himself down the hall toward the interrogation room. Even though he was tired, he knew there was work to be done and he wasn't the kind of cop to not do his job. He spoke to several other officers that passed by him as he walked down the hall. When he entered the interrogation room, he didn't recognize the man's face. He observed the track marks on his arms and the teardrop tattoo under his right eye. Both identifiers were an indication to Swift he was heavily involved in the street life. He was clearly under the influence of heroin. His eyes were closed and his head was less than an inch away from touching the table in front of him as it bobbed up and down. Swift slammed the door shut behind him and the young man jumped up because the sound startled him. Swift took a seat across from him to begin his investigation.

"I'm Detective Elvin Swift. I heard you were looking for me?" he asked bluntly.

"Yeah, it's about time you got here, man. I've been waiting for almost two hours in this bitch," the man stated with major attitude. He couldn't keep still in his seat. He wiped the slobber away from his mouth with the sleeve of his shirt. He looked worse for the wear. His clothes looked like they were three sizes too big for him. The jeans he had on were dusty and faded and his sneakers were filled with holes. Swift assessed he was probably in his mid to late thirties, but his drug abuse made him look twenty years older.

"What's your name, man?" Swift asked.

"My government name is Justin Nicks, but they call me Sticky on the streets because I'ma master thief. If it ain't nailed down around me, I will steal it from you. You can bet the house on that, bruh," he replied cockily with a proud chuckle.

"Sticky, have we met before because I can't place your face?" Swift shot back at him.

"Nah, we ain't met before, but I told them I only wanted to talk to the lead detective on this case. I want to make a confession about a murder I committed," he stated rather directed with a straight face.

"I'm listening. So who did you kill?" Swift asked him.

Based upon his physical appearance, Swift didn't believe he could hurt a fly. He had stared into the eyes of cold blooded killers on numerous occasions and Sticky didn't seem to have the outward demeanor of someone who fit that description. Swift had him pegged as nothing more than a petty thief and junkie who stole things to support his habit. He saw him as more of a danger to himself than anybody else. Nonetheless, he decided to hear him out because there was the possibility he could be wrong. It was a slim possibility, but a possibility nonetheless.

"I was breaking into this house in East Baltimore when the man that lived there came home. He ran up on me while I was trying to get away and I shot him in the chest several times. I didn't want to do it, but I had no choice. When he came at me, out of pure instinct, I just squeezed the trigger until the gun was empty. Since I killed him, his death has been weighing on my mind heavily. I'll admit that I'm a thief and I like to get high, but man I ain't no killer. This was just an accident. I wish I could take that night back," Sticky replied with tears in his eyes.

His teary eyed confession caught Swift off guard. It wasn't normal for someone to come into the police station and just confess to a murder. When Sticky gave him the address where the murder occurred, it struck a chord with Swift because it was an active investigation on his current caseload. The murder victim's name was Marcus Harrison. As he recalled the details of the case, he remembered the witness he interviewed identified a man and two females leaving the scene of the shooting. Sticky's story didn't match with the version of events that night given by Marcus' neighbor, Elias Knox, who claimed he heard Marcus arguing with a woman before he was shot. Also, the man seated in front of him also didn't fit the description given for the male suspect that Elias described. He knew something wasn't right with Sticky's story, but he decided to let him continue with his tale to see if he would slip up and reveal the truth as to what was really going on.

"You killed Marcus Harrison? Who else was involved in the crime with you because I was told there were two women on the scene as well," Swift stated in an attempt to get him to elaborate further.

"I don't know anything about any females being there. I was alone when I broke into his house. That's the whole truth," he stated rather firmly.

"This murder happened a minute ago. Why did you decide to turn yourself in now?" Swift inquired further. He tried again to get him to slip up in his story because he knew he was lying.

"It's like I told you, Officer. I have never killed anybody before. I know who I am and what I am and I accept that fact. I've had nightmares about that night. I keep seeing images of that kid in my dreams. I can't sleep at night man because of what I did," Sticky rambled on.

"Sticky, your story does not make any sense to me. Did somebody put you up to taking this charge? If they did, you can tell me. I've seen it too many times with guys like you when somebody pays you some money or threatens your life or the lives of your loved ones to make you take a charge. That's what this sounds like to me. You're not a killer like you said yourself, Sticky. Tell me the truth, man. I can help you. I would hate to see you go to jail for something you didn't do," Swift pressed him further. He noticed a brief hesitation from Sticky before he responded. That was the reaction he was looking for to prove his suspicion was correct.

"I'm not covering for anybody. I took a man's life and I deserve to be punished for what I did. That's my story, Detective. That's the truth. There's nothing more to add to it all. Now can we please get this over with so I can start serving my time," he replied vehemently.

"Well, I don't believe your story, but if you want to take this charge, then that's on you. I hope you have a change of heart because I would hate to see an innocent man go to jail. Justin Nicks, you're under arrest for the murder of Marcus Harrison. You have the right to remain silent. You have the right to an attorney. Anything you say can and will be used against you in a court of law," Swift rattled off to Sticky as he placed him into handcuffs. He led him out of the interrogation room so he could be processed for booking.

Swift was no longer sleepy anymore. The detective in him was wide awake. He was now intrigued because Sticky's confession was too good to be true. Even though he was adamant about his guilt and appeared to be sincerely traumatized by what he claimed to have done, it just didn't jibe with his gut instinct. The detective in him believed that someone put Sticky up to taking the charge, but he had no idea why. As far as he knew, Marcus was just a regular citizen with no important political or business connections to justify his murder being covered up. Until he was able to put the pieces to the puzzle together, he planned to let Sticky languish in prison based upon his own confession. This would be one less open murder on his caseload. His superiors would surely be pleased to receive this news.

Chapter 13

"Yeah, I know I'm the man. I can have any woman I want. Yeah, I look good. You want me don't you, girl? Yeah, you know you can't resist my charm," Jeremy rambled on as he glanced at himself in the mirror.

For most of his life, he had a hard time meeting women. He always got nervous and stuttered when he tried to approach a woman that he found attractive. Even though he was a wealthy man, his money didn't make up for his feelings of social inadequacy. The few women he spent time with recently were prostitutes he hired from different escort agencies he found online when he was up late at night web surfing. He didn't have to have a charming personality with them because as long as he had money to spend, they were down to have sex with him in any freaky way he desired. However, paying for sex grew tired for Jeremy. He longed for genuine female companionship where a woman enjoyed his company because of who he was as a person. When Cesare approached him about hanging out, he made his suggestion at just the right time in his life.

Currently, his level of self-confidence was through the roof. Thanks to Cesare's efforts to help him improve his self-image and appearance, he felt like he could get any woman he wanted. He had the money in the bank to flash to get their attention, but now he also had the swagger and style to match his net worth. After he spent a day out shopping with Cesare, Jeremy looked and felt like a new man. He replaced his horn rimmed glasses with a trendy pair of prescription Gucci spectacles. His new glasses made him look like a sophisticated college professor as opposed to a goofy oddball who didn't fit in any hip social circle. Cesare took him to Geno's personal tailor to have a few custom designed suits made. They also hit up all of the high end stores in Towson Town Center so he could pick up a few casual outfits to wear on the weekends. They made a trip to Cesare's barber so he could get a fresh haircut to replace his scraggly looking curly hairstyle.

When he looked at himself in the mirror, Jeremy liked what he saw. He no longer felt like the shy introvert he had been for all of his life. Cesare gave him a few lessons on how to approach a woman and he was ready to put his newly found charm to the test. He and Cesare had plans to hit the town tonight to party and have a good time after all of the hard work they put in at the office. Jeremy looked down at the new Michael Kors watch on his wrist and saw it was almost eight o'clock. Cesare would be at his place shortly to pick him up. He splashed on a dash of Invictus cologne before he exited his condo to make his way down to the lobby to wait for his ride. Cesare arrived right on time to pick him up.

"You're looking fly tonight, Jeremy. The ladies are going to be all over you," Cesare teased him as he hopped in the car.

"Thanks, Cesare. I appreciate you hooking me up with the fresh gear," Jeremy replied.

"Man, forget all of that mushy stuff. That's what friends do for each other. There's no need to thank me. That's enough of the serious talk. We're not at the office right now. Let's go have a good time tonight," Cesare stated excitedly.

Before Jeremy could respond, he adjusted the volume on his radio to increase the sound of the bass from the hip hop mixtape that played through the car stereo. He put the car in drive and sped off down the road while he bopped his head in tune with the beat of the music. It felt good for Cesare to have someone he could truly call a friend after the way Rah betrayed him. The subject of Rah was still a sore spot for him, but he knew he didn't have to worry about Jeremy doing the same thing. He looked forward to building a lasting friendship with him in addition to them both making a lot of money together in the process.

As they drove down the road, Jeremy started to feel more relaxed. He found himself vibing to the music. It felt good to finally be one of the cool guys for once after being looked at as a social outcast all of his life. As an only child, he spent most of his childhood alone, with very few friends. All throughout school he had it rough. Being the smartest kid in class made him feel uncomfortable around his classmates. They used to tease him and call him a geek all of the time which caused him to develop self-esteem issues. He would get chased home on a regular basis by the school bully. None of the girls gave him any play because of how homely he dressed. He didn't lose his virginity until his second year in college and it was to a fat girl named, Betsy, who was just as much of a geek as he was. All of his past misfortune was about to change. He wished all of the people who used to tease him could see him now. He was a successful millionaire business man. He couldn't wait to go to his high school reunion to rub it in their faces.

After about an hour on the road, they reached their destination in the northwest section of Washington, D.C. The club they were going tonight was a new spot called The Dirty Bar, located on

Connecticut Avenue. It was a trendy lounge where many of the hottest young professionals in the area got together to socialize and have a few drinks. The place could hold up to five hundred people and had a huge deck outside that was perfect for summer time partying. Cesare found the club online and wanted to try it out. When they pulled up in front of the club, all of the beautiful ladies in line took notice of Cesare's shiny BMW. They waited anxiously to see who the passengers inside were. When they stepped out of the car so the parking attendant could valet park the vehicle, all eyes were on them. Jeremy liked the attention. He felt like a superstar.

"Man, do you see all of these beautiful women out here? I'm ready to party tonight. Are you nervous?" Cesare asked.

It had been a good minute since Cesare went to a club. Ever since he changed his life and started working with Geno and going to school, he had little free time to have fun. He needed this night out on the town just as much as Jeremy did. He remembered how out of control he used to be when he was always high on marijuana when he used to go out to clubs in the past, but he was a different man today. He was more responsible and had different priorities in life than he did in his wilder days. He felt comfortable he could have a good time while exercising a greater level of self-control than he used to do in the past. He planned to put that theory to the test tonight.

"Nah, I'm okay, Cesare. I'm ready to mingle and have a few drinks with the ladies," Jeremy replied. Truth be told, he had butterflies in his stomach.

"I don't believe you, but just relax and follow my lead," Cesare instructed him.

They slowly made their way up to the front of the line to get inside of the club. Along the way, several beautiful women glanced in their direction. They played it cool and smiled back at them. When they reached the front door of the club, they were searched by security for weapons. After they were cleared by security, they went inside to pay the cashier. Once they were inside, Cesare led Jeremy straight to the bar. He ordered them both a Rum Runner, chased with a shot of Bacardi 151 rum. It was a strong drink and just what Jeremy needed to loosen up a little. He sipped it slowly while they made their rounds.

The music blasted through the speakers with the sounds of the latest hip hop hit records. Cesare bopped his head to the beat while Jeremy looked to be overwhelmed by the flashing lights and packed crowd. He had never been to nightclub before in his life. Cesare found a quiet section just off the dance floor for them to stand and observe the ladies while they danced. Cesare could tell the liquor had taken effect when Jeremy started dancing in tune with the rhythm of the music. After two more drinks, Jeremy's liquid courage was in full effect. He was bold enough to ask a young lady that caught his eye to dance. When she accepted his offer, he followed her to the dance floor and proceeded to get his groove on to the music. Cesare cheered him on from the sideline. After he danced with her for two songs, he made his way back over to the area where Cesare stood. The young lady he danced with went on about her way.

"Go ahead, playboy, I see you doing your thing. She was fine. You've got good taste, but why did you just let her walk away? Did you at least get her number?" Cesare asked.

"She was definitely hot. No, I didn't get her phone number because she said she had a man and was just here to have a good time. I'm not for the drama, Cesare," he replied.

"I can totally understand you on that one. Trust me; I have had my share of woman drama. Never mind her; do you see those chicks over there checking us out?" he yelled into Jeremy's ear so he could hear him over the loud music. Jeremy glanced in the direction Cesare pointed and observed three beautiful women by the bar with drinks in their hands. They were all dressed in short skirts and high heels. One of the females had shoulder length red hair, one was a platinum blonde with hair down to her buttocks, and the third one was a dark skinned, African American with a short cut hairstyle. When they noticed Jeremy and Cesare checking them out, they smiled back in their direction while they sipped their drinks.

"Yeah, I see them. Those chicks are banging," Jeremy replied. The 151 had him in a mellow, relaxed mood and ready to mingle.

"Let's go buy them some drinks. I want the Black girl with the nice ass. Yeah, I like my women chocolate and thick, brother," Cesare stated. It didn't matter to Jeremy which one he got because they all were good looking to him.

"I'm ready to roll. Let's do this," Jeremy said confidently.

They strolled through the crowd in the direction of the three young ladies. When they got closer to them, they did their best to play it cool as though they weren't just checking them out from across the room. However, Cesare saw right through their front and took the initiative to speak first.

"Excuse me miss, how are you doing tonight? My name is Cesare. It's nice to meet you," Cesare stated to the African American young lady. He extended out his arm to shake her hand and she returned the gesture. He wasn't the least bit bashful about making his choice known. His eyes stayed focused on her the whole time.

"I'm Danielle and these are my girls, Jazelle and Balyndah. It's nice to meet you," she replied. Judging by the way their eyes locked in on one another, it was clear the attraction was mutual.

"Does your friend speak for himself or is he the bashful type?" Balyndah, the busty blonde asked as she eyed Jeremy up and down.

"I absolutely can speak for myself. I'm Jeremy. It's nice to meet you, beautiful," he replied calmly.

"Fellas, that's enough of the small talk. Buy us some drinks so we can all have a good time tonight. You two look like you need to unwind a little bit," Jazelle interjected. Clearly she was the most outgoing member of the trio. She licked her lips while she playfully ran her hand along the collar of Jeremy's shirt. He eyed her body up and down and liked what he saw.

"That's a done deal," Cesare stated.

He grabbed the first waitress who walked past him and inquired about the cost of purchasing a VIP booth in the back of the club. When the waitress told him the price, Cesare reached into his pocket and pulled out a wad of cash to pay the required fee. Danielle looked like she wanted to have an orgasm when she saw his large bankroll. She grabbed onto his arm and joined him in following the waitress back to the VIP section. Jeremy had his hands full with Jazelle and Balyndah as he lagged closely behind them. They took turns groping him and he didn't resist one bit. It was clear by the body language displayed between two of them they were into some ultra freaky shit which was just what Jeremy needed in his life right now.

When they were all seated in their VIP booth, Cesare ordered several bottles of champagne and mixed drinks for all of them to drink throughout the rest of the night. As the alcohol took its effect, they all took turns alternating between the booth and the dance floor for the next few hours. It was almost three in the morning when they decided it was time to leave the club. Cesare suggested they all continue the party at his place and the ladies were down for his suggestion. He wasted no time in making his way up to the front of the club to retrieve his car. He was intoxicated, but not too drunk to drive home. The ladies all rode together to the club and proceeded to get their car as well so they could follow Cesare back to his place.

Chapter 14

Most homicide detectives would be excited
about being able to say they closed out a case
successfully even if all of the details didn't add it
up. More often than not, if they knew in their gut
the suspect was guilty, they would bend the rules if
necessary to ensure the suspect got what they
deemed to be his just due which would be a long
prison sentence. The means used to reach the
desired end were subjective, but the end result was
justifiable because it would result in another bad
guy being removed from the streets to no longer be
a menace to society. They would be even happier
about the conviction if the criminal actually
confessed to the murder without any form of police
coercion involved. To also have the murder weapon
in police custody would be the icing on the cake.
These two feathers in their caps made their job
that much easier. They wouldn't have to do as

much investigating on their own to search for witnesses or to find the murder weapon, both which routinely proved to be a trying and never ending task.

If a detective had enough successful convictions under his belt, over time, it would lead to upward mobility and career advancement within the ranks of the police department. To become a high ranking officer with a large salary and hefty pension plan appealed to most police officer and detectives, but not Elvin Swift. He was different from most. He marched to a different drummer. That was the reason why the Marcus Harrison case troubled him so and weighed heavily on his mind.

Being a police officer was more than just a job to Detective Swift. It was his life's purpose to serve the community and to try to do his part to make the streets of Baltimore as safe as possible for all of its citizens. He didn't cut corners or embellish his account of an arrest like he saw many of fellow officers do on numerous occasions. He did things by the book at all times. He always gave an honest account of events whenever he filed a report. That was why he was so respected by his fellow officers on the force as well as by citizens in the community. He treated people with respect and dignity whenever he was on a crime scene to question them about a case in an attempt to find witnesses to the crime. In all of his years on the force, he had never been charged with any form of misconduct or mistreatment of a suspect. Swift was an honorable guy and believed in the principles of freedom, justice, and equality for all. They were the principles by which he lived his life and conducted himself while on the job. To him, he was the same man in either setting.

Even though he had a signed confession from Sticky which stated he killed Marcus Harrison and he could close out the case, it didn't fit right with Detective Swift. The cop in him knew something wasn't right. Sticky's confession seemed staged like somebody put him up to taking the charge for reasons Swift didn't quite understand. His gut instinct told him there was more to this story than met the eye. It wasn't just a case of a robbery gone bad because when he read over the case files, there were no stolen items reported. Going further, Sticky's account of the killing didn't fit with the version of events described by Marcus' next door neighbor. His neighbor, Elias Knox, indicated there were three people on the scene and not a lone gunman involved in the killing. He specifically described hearing Marcus arguing with a female and not a male. It all just didn't add it up. He did his best to make Sticky break down and tell the truth, but he wouldn't budge from his story.

As things stood right now, Sticky was incarcerated and awaiting sentencing for a serious crime Swift knew he didn't commit. For him to have to serve a long jail sentence for somebody else didn't sit well with Swift. It was unjust, but he saw it happen more often than not in the streets of Baltimore. He had to at least try to make sense of this case to ease his own conscious. That was why he decided to make a trip over to Elias' house to follow up with him. He planned to get to the bottom of this case one way or another.

After he took Sticky's confession, he decided to do a little investigating of his own into his criminal background to see if it would give him any details to make this case make sense to him. When he did, he discovered that Sticky's rap sheet dated back over twenty years. He had arrests for charges such as petty theft, armed robbery, loitering, and CDS possession and possession with intent to distribute a CDS charges. He served multiple prison stints with the longest stretch being for three years. His criminal profile painted a picture of him being a drug addict who sold drugs on a small scale and stole to support his drug habit, but not that of a killer. It was consistent and matched the description Sticky gave of himself, but Swift still wasn't satisfied. He didn't believe Marcus' death was an accident because of the number of times he was shot. For him to have so many bullets pumped into his body by his killer pointed to a personal motive being the reason he was killed. The crime scene looked more like a crime of passion as opposed to a robbery that went wrong.

Swift also looked into Marcus Harrison's background and didn't find any history of criminal activity. In fact, he found evidence to support just the opposite. Everything he discovered about Marcus suggested he was just a young man who worked hard to support himself and to pay his way through college. When he checked into his finances, he saw he had a little over one thousand dollars in the bank and a small amount of credit card debt. He found no connection between him and Sticky that would make this case make sense. His investigation continued to push him further toward his belief there was something missing from this case he couldn't quite put his finger on.

When Swift pulled up to Elias' house, he parked his car out front and observed the surrounding area of his property. Nothing appeared to be out of the ordinary as he made his way up to the front steps. When he got to his front door, he noticed Elias' mailbox was overstuffed with mail as though it hadn't been checked in days. This sent up a red flag to Swift as he rang the doorbell. He waited for a few minutes, but got no response. He tried banging on the door, but the result was the same. When he looked into the front windows of the house, he didn't notice any movement inside. His instinct told him something wasn't right, but he decided to play it safe and just come back another day. He rationalized that maybe he was out of town visiting family or something. Consequently, he walked back to his car and was about to get inside when he heard a voice call out to him.

"Excuse me sir, are you looking for Elias? Can I talk to you for a minute?"one of Elias' neighbors yelled from her porch.

Swift closed his car door and walked toward the woman's house to see what she wanted. When he got closer he saw she was an elderly woman, in her late sixties, with a head full of grey hair. She had on a pair of reading glasses that hung down on the bridge of her nose. He walked up to the top of her steps to have a conversation with her.

"Hello, Ma'am, I'm Detective Elvin Swift. I was looking for your neighbor, Mr. Knox. I want to ask him a few questions. Have you seen him around?" he asked.

"My name is Hattie Mae Forrest. I know Elias very well. I knew his wife too before she passed away. We've all lived in this neighborhood for years. What do you want with Elias? Is this about that boy that got killed a while back? I told him to keep his mouth shut about what he saw. Lawd, I hope he's not in trouble," she rambled on. She appeared to be genuinely concerned about Elias' well being.

"Yes, this is about Marcus Harrison's murder. How well did you know him? What did Elias tell you about the case?" Swift asked.

"I didn't know the boy too well. I barely knew his father. He used to just speak and go about his business. He wasn't the sociable type. He didn't talk much. He died from cancer a few years ago and left Marcus that house. The boy was like his father in that he kept to himself, but he seemed like a good kid. I know he was in college before he died. It's so sad he had to die so young. Our young Black men are dropping like flies; honey child let me tell you. It makes me so sad to see things the way they are. Elias didn't tell me much about the murder except he saw the people who did it leaving out of the house," she stated in a moment of reflection. Swift got more information from Hattie Mae in five minutes than he did from anyone else in this entire investigation. She was clearly the neighborhood gossip who knew a little bit about everybody on the block's personal business. She might prove to be a valuable witness for him in the future.

"Are you sure he said he saw several people?" Swift asked to confirm Elias' statement he made to him the night he questioned him.

"Yes, he said he saw three people leaving out of the house. It was a man and two women. I might be old, honey child, but I ain't senile. I know what he told me," she shot back in a sassy tone.

"I apologize, Ms. Forrest. I meant you no disrespect. When was the last time you saw Elias?" he asked.

"I saw him about a week ago. He left out of his house like a bat out of hell. He had two suitcases in his hands. I called out to him to speak and he just waved. I saw him hop in a cab," she replied.

"Thank you very much, Ms. Forrest. You have been very helpful. If you see Elias and speak with him, can you have him to call me? Also, if you can think of any information that might prove to be useful, you can call me as well. Thank you for your time," Swift stated a he extended out his hand to give her his card. She glanced at it and put in her pants pocket.

As Swift walked away, he thought to himself that his suspicion was correct. There was more to this case than what was on the surface. When Ms. Forrest stated she saw Elias leave out of the house with suitcases, he knew the chances of him returning to his house were slim and none. He was in the wind either out of fear or somebody paid him off. Whatever the case might be, Swift was determined to get to the heart of the matter and solve the case. He knew his superior officers wouldn't approve of him continuing his investigation when they already had a confession from Sticky as well as the murder weapon. He would have to do this off the books on his own time. His focus now was on finding the suspects Elias identified.

Chapter 15

Cesare sat on the edge of his bed with both of his hands wrapped around his head. He wanted to scream in agony because had an unbearable headache. His temples were filled with an intense throbbing pain he hadn't experienced in quite some time. All of the liquor he consumed the night before and into the wee hours of the morning made him feel nauseous. His stomach did somersaults and back flips. He wanted to vomit, but he was too dizzy to make it to the toilet. He glanced at the clock on his nightstand and was shocked to see it was one o'clock in the afternoon. He was glad it was Saturday because if this was a work day, he would be in a boat load of trouble with Geno for being so late to work.

When he stopped smoking weed and got more serious about his life, he swore he wouldn't have any more wild adventures partying like he did last night anymore. When he came to work for Geno and enrolled in school, he told himself his days of having one night stands was over. However, just like it was with most things people enjoyed in life that were bad for them, all it took was a brief moment to forget about the pain and long term effects and to remember the good side of things before one could find himself right back into the mix.

When he glanced over his shoulder and got a glimpse of the plump, dark skinned ass on Danielle stretched out in his bed, he understood why it was so easy for him to lose focus. She had a body that could make a priest lose his religion. Danielle was so amazing when it came to oral sex Cesare almost wanted to pay her for her services. The freaky things she did to him last night justified in his mind the suffering he would endure until his headache went away. However, he made a vow to himself this was a one night thing and he planned to stick to his word from here on out. Time would tell how long his pledge would last.

Cesare waited a few minutes before he got up and made his way to the bathroom. He bolted from the bed to the toilet because his bladder was so full he almost urinated on himself. When he finally made it over to the toilet, he peed for what seemed like an eternity. Once he was done, it felt like an immense burden had been lifted from his shoulders. He walked over to the sink and pulled one of the small Dixie cups out of the dispenser next to it and filled it with water. Next, he reached inside of his medicine cabinet and grabbed a packet of Alka-Seltzer pain relief tablets. When he dropped the tablets into the water and heard the familiar fizzing sound they made, he knew relief was on the way. When he used to be a heavy drinker, Alka-Seltzer was the perfect medicine to take away his pain the next day. It never failed him. Once the fizzing sound stopped, he put the cup to his lips and gulped down the home remedy. It would take a few minutes before it took effect. He walked back into his bedroom.

"Hey, handsome, what are you doing up so early? When I woke up and didn't see you I was worried. I thought I wore you out last night," she teased him.

Cesare was surprised to see Danielle was awake already after all the liquor she drank and cocaine she snorted the night before. She inhaled the coke like her nose was a vacuum cleaner. She tried to get him to indulge with her, but he declined. Cesare already gave up using marijuana, his drug of choice, and had no intention of developing a new drug habit. The fact she was so heavy into hard drugs let him know off the bat she could be no more than a one night stand for him. He didn't need a setback to undue all of the positive strides he had made in his life recently.

Danielle was wrapped up in the sheets with her head propped up on the pillows. She glanced at him with a big smile on her face. The way he sexed her last night had her sprung. Cesare wasn't feeling the look she gave him because he knew it too well. He hoped she wasn't getting any big ideas about them hooking up again because it wasn't going to happen. Last night was fun, but Cesare wasn't looking for a girlfriend. He just wanted to have a good time with no strings attached. The star struck look she had on her face when she eyed his naked body up and down suggested she had something else on her mind. He vaguely remembered, in between all of the alcohol, her telling him she loved him a few times during several of the steamy sex sessions they had. Being in love was the last thing on his mind right now. If she had any ideas about them being in a relationship, Cesare planned to nip that it in the bud quickly.

Danielle let out a loud yawn and stretched out her arms. In the midst of her stretching, the bed sheet happened to fall off of her. Her voluptuous figure was on full display. Cesare couldn't help but to notice how thick she was. She had a butt like Serena Williams with a slim waist. Her thighs were thick and nicely toned. Her face was just as appealing as the body. He had a flashback of how she looked when he had her in the doggy style position last night. He reminisced about how turned on he got when her ass giggled every time he stroked her from behind. The memory had him thinking he might have to go another round with her before she left.

"Yeah, you did your thing last night, lady. I can't lie about that at all. You put it on me without a doubt," Cesare admitted.

"I'm glad you enjoyed yourself. You know I don't normally give a guy some on the first night, but I was really feeling you. I'm not freaky like this with every guy I date. It's something about you that made me want to go there with you. I mean you are a good looking man, but it's more to it than that why I'm so attracted to you, Mister. I'm really digging your swagger. You've got a little soul in you for a White boy," she teased him.

"Is that right? Well, this White soul brother thanks you for the compliment. I'm flattered," Cesare responded humbly. Judging by the serious look on her face, his response didn't sit too well with Danielle.

"You're flattered? Is that all you have to say after I gave you all of this good stuff? You don't have to play the tough guy role with me. I know you want some more of this. I got it bad for you too, Mr. Caprese. I think I want to keep you for myself. You play your cards right and I might just make you my man," she stated rather forthright.

Danielle didn't have a hidden agenda. She put her cards right on the table. She wanted to claim Cesare and wasn't the least bit bashful about her intentions. She was the kind of female who liked to control the men she got involved with intimately. That wouldn't work too well with Cesare because he wasn't the type of man to be controlled by a woman. This conversation was headed in a direction Cesare sought to avoid. He had to be careful how he chose his words because if he said the wrong thing, this whole situation could go way left for him.

Cesare had flashbacks of his situation with Princess and how it almost ruined his life. He didn't want a repeat of all of that drama. He had to do damage control and find an easy way to let Danielle down. Being realistic about the situation, he had just met her last night at the club, they had a night filled with wild sex, and here she was talking about being in a relationship. She had all of the tell tale signs of a psycho chick. He had no desire for an emotional attachment to a woman anytime soon. Ever since Princess' tragic accidental death, Cesare thought it was best for him to stay single for awhile. Even though they argued all of the time, he genuinely loved her and she loved him. Her death changed everything for Cesare. He saw the world and his place in it differently. He was more mature and focused. Last night was an anomaly. He just wanted to get his freak on and nothing more.

"I appreciate your honesty, Danielle. I had a good time last night and I see you did too. However,

I'ma keep it real with you. I'm not really looking for a girl right now. I've got a lot going on in my life and I don't have the time for a relationship," he told her honestly.

"I hear what you're saying, but I want you to hear what I'm saying. I'm not used to a man turning me down and I always get what I want. You can have your space for now, but when it's all said and done, you will be all mine," she said. Clearly, Cesare's attempt to let her down easy flew right over her head.

"Hold on to that thought. I'ma be right back. I'm going to go and check on Jeremy to see how he's doing. I hope your girls didn't put it on him too bad," Cesare stated brushing off her delusional rant.

He quickly threw on a pair of shorts and a tank top and made a quick beeline for the door. He left Danielle and all of her craziness to stew in her twisted thoughts. If she really believed she was going to make him her man, she needed to wake up and face reality. Cesare wasn't about to let that happen. He thought to himself how he was going to get this crazy chick out of his condo without any drama.

When he reached the living room, he had to forget about his dilemma for a minute. The sight of Jeremy passed out on his sofa with Balyndah and Jazelle nude made him feel proud. Judging by all of the bottles of liquor spread across the floor and the way their clothes were scattered about the room, it was clear to him Jeremy had a good time. A threesome with two hot chicks was just what he needed to finally start to enjoy life and not devote as much of his time to work. Cesare's mission was accomplished and it made last night worthwhile. He just had to make sure Jeremy didn't make more of the good time he had with them than it really was. It was just sex and nothing more. As for Danielle, he had to find a way to get rid of her so she didn't become a problem.

Chapter 16

Gianna had more clothes inside of her walk-in closet than the law should allow for any teenager to own. However, she wasn't just any teenager. She was the daughter of Geno Caprese and he spoiled her to no end by buying her whatever she wanted. All day shopping sprees with her mother were a normal occurrence in her young life. With a budding career in the modeling world, she had to dress the part at all times. She studied endlessly all of the hottest fashion magazines so she could stay up to date on the latest styles in fashion. She knew what was hot and what was not and Geno made sure she stayed draped in the trendiest gear. All she had to do was come to him with the puppy dog eyes look and Geno would be putty in her hands. He never turned her down no matter how much of his hard earned money she wanted to blow. She was his baby girl and would always be that even when she was grown. Besides, the more money he spent only gave him added motivation to go out and make some more. His children were accustomed to the finer things in life and he wouldn't have them live any other way.

"Mommy, I need your help! Where are you?" she yelled at the top of her lungs from her bedroom.

Her parent's bedroom was at the far end of the hallway, but Gianna was determined to be heard. Gianna was in a panic because she couldn't find her favorite pink shirt. She wore a hole in the carpet in her bedroom as she raced back and forth in an effort to pinpoint its location. She had looked everywhere; from her closet to under her bed to even behind her dresser, but it was nowhere to be found. She tossed her dirty laundry basket, but it wasn't there either. Carina appeared in the doorway of Gianna's room minutes later to find out why she screamed her name so loudly.

"Gianna, have you lost your mind, young lady? Why are you yelling so loud?" Carina asked.

"Mommy, have you seen my pink Gucci shirt? Did you move it? I can't find it anywhere?" she asked in return.

"You're making all of that noise over a lousy shirt with all of those clothes you have in your closet? To answer your question, no, I didn't move your shirt," Carina replied.

"Oh, Mom, you just understand. What am I going to do? I wanted to wear that shirt so bad," Gianna whined.

"What you better do is find something else to wear. You also better clean this mess up before you leave out of here," Carina uttered in her most stern parental voice.

"Okay, Mom, I will," Gianna promised her before she walked back down the hallway to rejoin Geno in the master bedroom.

Gianna knew she better do what her mother asked or she would be punished because Carina didn't play around when it came to her following her directions. Frustrated, Gianna took her mother's advice and gave up her search because thus far it had proven to be waste of time and effort. It took her a good fifteen minutes inside of her walk-in closet perusing through her large wardrobe before she settled on an alternative. She found an orange print shirt to wear. She put it up against the designer jeans she planned to wear and observed the outfit in her full sized mirror to make sure her ensemble was to her liking. Satisfied with her selection, she quickly got dressed.

She had plans to go to the movies with her girlfriends and then to spend the weekend at her best friend Pia's house. She had looked forward to this girl time all week and didn't want anything to get in the way of her plans. After she was fully

dressed, she proceeded to clean her room as her
mother instructed her to do.

While Gianna was busy getting ready for her
weekend with her girlfriends, Stefan was down the
hall in his bedroom stuffing his book bag with all of
his favorite action figures and video games. Carina
had already packed his clothes for him in a
separate bag. He too had plans for the weekend. He
planned to spend the weekend over his best friend
Paul's house. He and Paul went to the same school
and were in the same grade. They also played on
the same baseball team in the summer time. Geno
already had John Lucci do a thorough background
check on his parents and they met with his
approval so he felt comfortable with Stefan staying
over at their home. Of course, he would have his
own security guards stationed just outside of their
residence for Stefan's added protection. The same
held true for Gianna. She had her own security
detail that followed her everywhere she went. To be
the children of such a powerful and wealthy man
like Geno made them a target for the rest of their
lives. Geno did his best to ensure their safety. He
planned to have Clay drop them off at their
separate destinations while he remained home with
Carina so they could spend some alone time
together.

To have a quiet moment alone with his wife
and to not have to worry about receiving a call from
one of his clients or having to make some important

business decision was a rare occasion for Geno. Tonight appeared to be the perfect opportunity for him to have some romantic alone time with Carina. Geno decided to cut the ringer off on his phone off and to not take any calls. He didn't want any distractions. He wanted to enjoy his wife and give her his undivided attention because she deserved it from him. He wanted to revel in her beauty and enjoy the pleasure of her company. Every now and then he needed a reminder to fully appreciate the awesome woman he had by his side. She was the best mother and partner in crime he could have ever asked to have in his life to help him fulfill his destiny. Carina cherished their quality time together just as much, if not more. To lie in the arms of her King was the most comfortable and secure place for her to be on this Earth.

After Clay arrived to pick up Gianna and Stefan, Geno and Carina had the entire house to themselves to do whatever they pleased. Their argument from the other day was a distant memory. Even though she felt Geno was wrong for not going to see his father, Carina couldn't stay mad at him forever. Geno couldn't stay mad at her either. The love between the two of them overcame any disagreement they ever had.

Since they had some alone time, they decided to catch a movie together in their theater room. The two lovers were snuggled up closely as they watched *Focus*, Will Smith's latest flick. The onscreen chemistry between Smith and his leading lady, actress Margot Robbie, was magical but paled in comparison to the real world sparks generated by Geno and Carina. They were total opposites of one another in terms of personality style, but together they comprised a powerful team. With Geno in the role of the larger than life and highly intelligent, but deadly gangster and Carina as the strong, supportive backbone of their family, if their story were turned into a film it could hold its own with any of the greatest love stories ever produced on film in Hollywood. It would surely generate millions of dollars at the box office and be a smashing success because nearly all Americans loved a realistic love story filled with drama and excitement.

While the movie played up on the large three hundred inch screen, the two of them alternated between moments of laughter and moments of anxiety. They eagerly anticipated what drama awaited the two main characters, Nicky and Jesse Barrett, from scene to scene. Both actors did an outstanding job in bringing their characters to life. When it finally came to an end about two hours later, they both could honestly say they enjoyed every minute of the movie. As the credits rolled, Carina laid her head on Geno's shoulder.

"That movie was good, honey, but the company was even better," Carina stated in reference to him.

Before he could respond, she leaned over and stole a kiss. She got even bolder when she got up out of her seat and sat in his lap. She lifted up her dress and spread her legs across his to get more comfortable. Geno didn't resist her advances not one bit. He loved it when she chose to be the aggressor. It felt good to be able to not be the one in charge all of the time. Besides, he was eager to see what else Carina had in store for him.

"I feel the same way about you, my love. You do know what you're doing to me sitting right there, don't you?" Geno asked her flirtatiously. Her crotch pressed up against his gave him an instant erection. When he wrapped his arms around her waist and pulled her closer toward him, his level of arousal further increased.

"I absolutely do know what I'm doing. I see your little friend down there doesn't mind either," Carina teased him. She grinded her hips on his manhood and found herself getting more and more turned on. Geno's hands now began to explore her body. He placed his hands on her derriere and held it tightly. Thoughts of all the nasty things he wanted to do to her raced through his mind. It had been a long time since they got freaky in the theater room and they planned to make the most of the moment.

"Damn, you taste good, woman," Geno uttered while his tongue danced across her neck and made its way onto her chest. Her sweet scent tantalized his nostrils. The softness of her flesh invited him to explore more parts of her body. He ripped open her blouse and helped her undo her bra so her breasts were fully exposed. Carina's heart raced as a result of his unexpected sexual aggression. When he lifted up her bra and took her breasts into his mouth, her sweet spot exploded in his lap and left a wet spot on his pants. Geno didn't mind at all. In fact, he was thrilled to know he still got her that excited after so many years of marriage.

Geno had a look on his face like he wanted to just rip her clothes off and ravage her body from head to toe. Carina read his mind and decided to help him out by fulfilling his fantasy. She stood up, undid the zipper on the back of her dress, and let it fall to the floor. Geno's eyes were mesmerized by her beauty. She stood before him in nothing but her bikini underwear. The sight was breathtaking to say the least. Even after she had children, Carina's body still enticed him enough to want to make love over and over again.

"Let me dance for you," Carina stated seductively.

"By all means, you do whatever you desire, my love," Geno stated rather calmly. Carina never ran out of sexy surprises to keep his attention. She had Geno pussy whipped.

Carina didn't need any music in the background to dance for her man. Her hips gyrated from side to side in tune with the rhythm of her heartbeat as it raced inside of her chest. Just the thought of what it would feel like to have Geno inside of her created a melody inside of her head that kept her on beat. Geno's eyes were locked in on her every movement. He relaxed back in his chair and undid his pants to fully expose himself for her to see. He wanted her to know what effect she had on him. While one hand was wrapped around his manhood, he motioned to Carina with his free hand for her to come to him.

"That's enough of this teasing bullshit, Carina. I want you now, woman," Geno stated rather primitively. He felt like a beast ready to feast upon his prey. He couldn't wait any longer to have Carina.

"I see somebody is eager to be a little naughty tonight. Is that all for me?" Carina asked playfully as she glanced at his stiffness with nothing but lust in her eyes. Geno nodded his head to confirm her notion. Carina walked over to him to do her own personal feel test. Once she had Geno's manhood in the palms of her hand, she went a step further and took him into her mouth. His head rocked back and rested against the headrest of the chair while her head went up and down in his crotch area. All Geno could do was moan, close his eyes, and just enjoy the moment. When he felt himself about to explode, he pushed her head away abruptly.

"Come sit on it, now," he demanded.

Carina got up from off of her knees and climbed back into his lap with her backside facing toward him. Geno helped her pull her underwear down. When he inserted himself inside of her, Carina hips instinctively began to do a grinding motion which further aroused Geno. He planted passionate kisses all over her back while his hands massaged her clitoris. Carina moaned and begged for him not to stop. His fluid motions made her body become submissive to his dirty thoughts. He could do whatever his imagination wanted to do with her right now. Geno turned up the flames of passion when he got up from his seat and threw Carina down in the chair forcefully. He spread her legs and entered her with his member. As he glanced at Carina, he got more turned on by the sexy facial expressions she made every time he thrust himself inside of her. She pulled his body down on top of hers so she could feel every inch of him between her thighs.

"Keep it right there, Geno. Yeah, just like that, baby. You're hitting my G spot, baby. Ohhh, I want to come for you. Make me come, Geno," she begged.

Eager to switch things up and give her what she asked for, Geno lifted Carina out of the chair and turned her around. He positioned himself behind her. She bent over to grab a hold of the chair. They went at it from the doggy style position for a solid fifteen minutes before Geno couldn't hold back his orgasm any longer. He just closed his eyes and braced himself for the ultimate moment of ecstasy. The sensual emotions that ran through Carina's being when he came reminded her why she loved this awesome man so much.

Geno knew where touch her to make her weak. He knew how to stroke her just right to make her become a submissive sex slave. Geno trained Carina how to be everything he wanted his wife to be in the bedroom and she was a willing student. The Caprese theater room was usually reserved for watching movies. However, tonight there was enough steamy action for them to make their own home movie. By the time they were done making love, they had created an epic memory to be savored for eternity.

"Geno, that was amazing. We haven't had sex like that in a long time," Carina confessed while she collapsed in his arms.

"Yes, it has been a minute. It's good to know that after all of these years my baby still has a little freak inside of her that she's been saving for Daddy," Geno teased her in reference to the naughty little dance routine she performed for him. He loved the way her body moved especially when she was naked.

"I'll do anything to keep you happy, Geno Caprese. You're the love of my life," Carina confessed. She meant what she said. His wish was her desire. She aimed to please her man royally.

She knew if she kept him happy in the bedroom, he would be more focused in the board room when he conducted business.

"And you, Carina Caprese, are my muse. You're my ultimate inspiration. This was my way of making it up to you for the crazy way I acted the other day when you tried to talk some sense into me when I was really acting childish about the situation with my father. You were right, baby, I'm going to go see him. He's still my father and I do love him. I think that's the reason what he did hurt so much," Geno replied honestly. He knew her worth to his life so there was no need for him to pretend. She could get through to him to make him see the error in his ways when no one else could. He was the baddest gangster Baltimore City ever saw, but he would be a wreck without her as a part of his foundation. She was his rock. His statement made Carina blush. Every now and then she needed to hear him tell her how much she meant to him.

"I'm glad you reached that decision. It's for the best. Since you found out about your other brother and sister, have you reached out to them? "she inquired. Geno hesitated before he responded.

"Yes, I've made contact with Jericho. Actually, he reached out to me, but I have yet to meet Shavon," he replied.

"How did it go?" she asked.

"It was a brief, cordial conversation. I told him a few things I felt he should know. Leonardo's absence from his life has left him feeling some type of way, but I told him that shouldn't interfere with us developing a relationship. We agreed to speak again," he replied half truthfully.

"I'm proud of you for letting go of those bad feelings. I just want to say one thing else and I will leave this subject alone. Your mother mentioned to me that your father wants to see all of his children one last time. Can you do your best to make that happen?" she asked.

"I'll do my best for you," he replied honestly.

"That's all you can do is try, Geno," Carina replied.

"That's enough of the serious talk. You're killing my mood. I'm almost ready for round two," Geno stated to change the subject. He wasn't being inconsiderate. He was just horny and ready to enjoy more quality adult time with his wife. Before Carina had a chance to respond, Geno found his second wind and got up from his chair. He lifted Carina up in his arms and carried her up the stairs in route to their bedroom.

Chapter 17

While Jericho was in the living room with Gutta discussing business, Shavon was in the bedroom in her pajamas with Nina watching the movie *Brown Sugar* for the umpteenth time while she ate a bowl of Fruit Loops. It was her all time favorite movie. She had watched the movie so many times she had the lines committed to memory. She had the biggest crush on Taye Diggs ever since when she was a teenager. She used to fantasize about him being her boyfriend when she grew up. When she got older, she hoped to find her own tall, dark and handsome knight in shining armor to call her own. She thought Marcus was going to be the one, but she never imagined she could be so wrong. She had no idea he could go from being such a sweet guy to turning into a violent, predatory monster. Because of him, falling in love was the furthest thing from her mind. Her perception of true love was now tainted.

As things stood currently, Shavon was in a battle to regain her sanity and to try to begin living a normal life again. She went from being a paralegal with aspirations to one day become a lawyer to a broken young woman trying to pick up the pieces of her fractured life. It was a daily struggle. She did the best she could to become her old self again. There were days she felt fine and in a good mood where she would be joking and laughing with Jericho and Shavon and then there were days when the images of her attack crept back out of her subconscious mind and made her want to stay in bed all day and just cry because she felt so violated. Lately, she had experienced more good days than bad, which was an indication she was making some progress along her road to recovery.

While she enjoyed the movie, Shavon had the pillows propped up against the headboard behind her to make her feel more comfortable. Nina was stretched out across the bottom of the bed almost half asleep. The wear and tear of caring for Shavon, with all of her sleepless nights and unpredictable emotional outbursts, had her drained. She didn't complain because she loved Jericho enough to do whatever was necessary to make sure his little sister was taken care of properly. Jericho had done the same thing caring for her when he rescued her from the streets many years ago. It was only right she returned the kindness he showed her to his baby sister. Their love might have been unconventional, but it was tried and true. She would be right there by Shavon's side no matter how long it took for her to get better.

"Nina, are you sleeping?" Shavon asked in between chomping down on the Fruit Loops cereal.

"No, I'm up, Shavon. What's on your mind? What do you need me to do, honey?" she asked in return. She lifted her head off of the bed and turned around to face Shavon.

"I don't need you to do anything for me. I just wanted to tell you I was sorry for giving you such a hard time for so long. You're good for my brother. He needs you in his life," she uttered.

"Where did that come from, Shavon? What made you say that?" she asked curiously.

She thought about all of the back and forth bickering they used to do for the longest time. Shavon had done everything in her power to break her and Jericho up because she felt Nina wasn't good enough for him. Nina would be right back at her throat to defend herself in justifying why she deserved to be in Jericho's life. Nina had waited for so long to gain her approval of their relationship. To hear those words finally was pleasing to her soul.

"My brother and I have been through a lot. When our mother died, it changed him inside. Even though I know he loves me and would do anything for me, I can see a lot of hatred and pain in his eyes because he is bitter about how she died. There's a hole in his soul that he fills doing what he does, killing people. Yes, I know what he does for a living even though he has always tried to hide it from me to protect me. I'm not a fool by a long shot. I don't judge him, but I want him to stop before he gets hurt or goes to jail. Jericho is smart. He has already made a lot of money doing the wrong things and I just want him to take his money and do something different today. He can do whatever he sets his mind to doing. I need your help, Nina. We've got to get him to see that he can have a normal life. I don't want to lose him and I know you don't either. He has always been there to take care of me, but I think it's time I take care of him," Shavon elaborated.

"Shavon, you just blew my mind with what you just said. I need time to process it all. I just don't know what to say right now," Nina stated sincerely.

She couldn't believe what she just heard come out of her mouth. For the past few months, she and Jericho were worried about Shavon's sanity and she just made the most clear headed statement. Her words echoed what Nina felt inside about Jericho for quite some time now. Nina was even more optimistic than ever that Shavon had started to come back to her normal self. She couldn't wait to share the news with Jericho.

"I'm just being honest with you, Nina. I mean look at what you've done for me. You could have just left Jericho to take care of me alone, but you didn't. You've stayed right by my side through all of my ups and downs dealing with Marcus raping me. I'm just now starting to feel like myself again. Just for me to be able to say he raped me and not feel like it was my fault is a big step for me. I now I need to talk to a psychiatrist because I still have a lot of things to work through. I just want you to know how much I appreciate everything you've done for us. What I'm trying to say is I love you like a sister, Nina," Shavon said with tears in her eyes.

"I love you too, Shavon. You are right about everything. I want your brother to stop doing what he is doing too, but I think he gets a sick thrill out of killing people. He doesn't just do it for the money. He has more than enough cash saved up for us to live well for a long time. I've watched him and see how he acts after he has completed a job. He is calm and acts normal as though he didn't just kill someone. It's like his emotions are a light switch he turns off and on when he feels like it. I love him with all of my heart and I don't want to get a phone call one day telling me to come identify his body. It would crush my heart," Nina confessed. Her love for Jericho was nothing but sincere. Her eyes began to water at just the thought of not having Jericho around. She couldn't envision not being able to be held by his strong, comforting arms every night.

"We've got to find a way to get him some help, Nina. I know I need help, but he does too. We're both messed up. We've got to work together to do this because I don't want to lose my brother and I know you don't either," she stated passionately. Shavon got up from under the covers and gave Nina a hug. They both cried on each other's shoulders.

"Look at us getting all mushy up in here. I guess watching this movie and seeing Taye Diggs and Sanaa Lathan's characters fall in love got us all emotional, huh?" Nina joked.

"Yeah, I guess so," Shavon replied while she wiped the tears from her eyes. They both lay down at the top of the bed and continued to enjoy the movie. Words couldn't truly capture how either of them felt inside right now. When the movie was almost at the end, Jericho happened to appear in the doorway.

"What's going on here? Are y'all bonding? Is this a love fest I see?" he joked. He had no clue he was just the topic of their conversation.

"Are you jealous because my sister and I are bonding?" Shavon teased him. She too had a big smile on her face. It had been so long since Jericho saw it that he forgot how beautiful it truly was. It gave him hope his little sister was on her way back to him.

"I'm not jealous at all. I'm happy to see you two getting along. I just wanted to see if you needed anything before I left out to take care of some business," he replied. He was headed to the store do some shopping for some supplies he needed to complete his next assignment.

"No we don't need anything, but we did want to talk to you about some things. Come have a seat," Shavon requested.

"What do you want to talk about?" Jericho asked. He plopped down in the motorized recliner chair across from the bed.

"Well, I guess I'll go first. We were just talking and we're both concerned about you, baby. We want you to get out of the business you're in with Gutta. It's time. You've made enough money for us to live a good life. You don't need to kill people anymore, baby. Please stop," Nina pleaded with him.

"Jericho, I feel the same way. I want you to take your money and start some kind of business or something. You're smart. Anything you put your mind and heart into you will be good at without a doubt. This whole situation has had me thinking a lot about how precious life is. Even when you guys might have thought I was crazy, I had my moments of clarity, but I just kept them to myself. I thought about what life would be like if we all wound up going to jail. I thought about how I would feel if I got a call one day to come identify your body, Jericho. If you thought getting rape crushed me, I would lose my mind without you. I've depended on you my entire life. Ever since Mommy died, you've been there for me every step of the way. What I'm saying is I need my big brother. If you love, you will think about what we are asking you to do," Shavon interjected before Jericho even had a chance to respond to Nina's comments. They figured if they both tag teamed him, it might pressure him to consider their request. They thought it was the best shot they had to make him change his lifestyle.

"Where is all this coming from out of the blue?" Jericho asked feeling overwhelmed. He was an Alpha male who always did things on his time. He didn't like to feel pressured into making a decision.

"It's been building up inside of me for quite some time now. Jericho, you've been lucky this far not to get caught doing what you're doing. You've gotten rich from it and I just think it's time to quit while you still have a chance to do so," Nina replied.

"Let's be clear about one thing: I haven't gotten caught not because I've been lucky, but it's because I've been careful and cautious with every step I take. I'm good at what I do. Hell, I'm the best at what I do. Have you ever considered this is what I was born to be?" Jericho asked.

"That's nonsense, Jericho. Stop talking foolishly. Nobody was put on this Earth for the purpose of killing people. That's ridiculous. It's wrong and eventually it will catch up to you," Shavon countered his argument.

"Well, I guess if I'm going to hell for killing people, at least I know I won't be alone," he shot back as he glanced at Nina. As soon as the words left out of his mouth, he knew he made a mistake. He let his emotions get the best of him. Nina shot an evil stare in his direction. He knew she was pissed off. He glanced in Shavon's direction for a nod of support, but she was just as upset with him because of the ignorant comment he just made.

"I'm done talking about this subject. Do what you want to do, Jericho. It's your world. We just live in it to serve you and your needs. It's clear how we feel doesn't matter," Nina stated emotionally.

"Can we talk about this at another time?" he asked. He was eager to get to work on plotting out his next kill.

Jericho wanted to apologize for what he said, but he figured it would fall on deaf ears at the moment. Instead of making matters worse and saying something else he couldn't take back, he decided to quit while he was ahead.

"Yeah, it can wait. Jericho, please be careful out there," Nina replied. Even though he was acting like an ass right now, she still loved him.

Their love was unconditional. She could tell by the look in his eyes what he was about to do. Every time he took on a new assignment, she prayed he returned to her in one piece.

"I always am. You don't have to worry about me, baby. I'll be back soon," Jericho responded.

He got up out the chair and exited the room. He closed the door behind him. He had a brief conversation with Gutta about his next assignment before he left out of the door. While he walked to the car, Jericho felt some relief to see Shavon making some improvement in her mental condition. Even though she wasn't out of the woods yet, any positive change was better than him seeing her as frazzled as she was just a few weeks ago. He couldn't explain why all of sudden she began to display flashes of her old self, but he didn't care. He just hoped her progress continued until he was able to get her the professional help she needed. Just as he was about to pull off in his car, he got a text message from a number he didn't recognize. When he read the message, he knew who it was. He let out a sigh of relief. It was Geno. He had delivered as promised.

Chapter 18

  With all of the hard work he put in to become a rich man, every now and then Geno deserved to enjoy the spoils of his wealth and to share it with his closest associates. One of his guilty pleasures he took pride in was the Club Level executive suite he leased at the Verizon Center in Washington, D.C., so he could enjoy watching the Washington Wizards, his favorite NBA team, play basketball all season long in the most luxurious accommodations his money could buy. His suite came with two dozen complimentary tickets and a fully catered buffet of food and alcohol for him and his guests to enjoy. There were several rows of theater seats as well as comfortable bar stools for him and his guests to sit in while they watched the game. There was a large kitchen area equipped with a full sized refrigerator as well as a private restroom. What he loved the most about the suite was the convenience and privacy it allowed him and his guests to have. They didn't have to deal with long lines at the concession stands or public bathrooms because the suite accommodated all of their needs. If any of his guests wanted something special that wasn't on the menu, Geno would make sure the catering staff fulfilled their request.

Geno would settle for nothing less than the best for himself and those he considered to be like family to him. Since they all worked hard and were good earners, it was only right he reward them in a proper way. Whatever Geno did, he did it with style and class. He set the bar high for himself and those individuals in his social circle.

Tonight's game was against the Oklahoma City Thunder. Even though he was a diehard Wizards fan, Geno couldn't help but cheer for the Thunder at times because he was a big fan of their top player, Kevin Durant. It was an added bonus that he happened to be from the Maryland/ Washington D.C. area. With Durant and Russell Westbrook teamed up together, the Thunder had a chance to win the NBA title every year. They were an exciting team on the court, but he was more impressed by the front office moves made by their general manager, Sam Presti.

Geno loved the way he developed the team's core around a group of players with raw talent and athleticism and created a bond between them that was rock solid. They didn't just look at each other as teammates who played night in and night out for just the big paychecks and the fame. They were a family and played with pride to be able to represent Oklahoma City and its fans. The core values that Presti used to build the Thunder team were similar to the values Geno used to build the Caprese Foundation. His top lieutenants were his family. When he ate, they ate. He would ride or die for them and they would all do the same for Geno. Loyalty and upstanding character was as important to Geno as it was to the Oklahoma City Thunder front office. If the head of an organization stood for solid principles, then all of its parts would fall in line and the organization would run perfectly like a well-oiled machine.

"Whoa, did you see John Wall just take Westbrook to the hole? That boy is on fire!" Milton yelled as he sipped his beer. He had a plate full of Buffalo wings and fries in front of him.

"That's okay because Westbrook is about to return the favor. I see a facial coming on the next play! Just wait for it!" Jarvis countered.

He was a big OKC Thunder fan while Milton was a big Wizards supporter. They went back and forth all of the time talking trash to each other. He got up from his seat and exchanged a high five with Moreno, who brought two of his young groupies with him to the game. He had one of them seated on each of his legs while he reclined in the theater chair. Geno didn't mind him bringing his guests with him. He just wanted them all to have a good time.

Sal and Geno were seated in the front row of the theater seats enjoying the game. Cesare and Jeremy sat behind them. Jeremy was happy Geno invited him because this was a new experience for him. He didn't know much about basketball, or any other sports for that matter. He was just happy to be a part of the in crowd after being an outsider for most of his life. He truly appreciated the gesture. He brought Balyndah along with him as his guest.

Cesare planned to bring one of his female friends to the game with him, but opted against it when he found out who Jeremy intended to bring. All he needed was for Balyndah to report back to Danielle she saw him with another female and the drama would soon follow. Ever since that one night he spent with her when they first met, she called him consistently trying to hook up, but he never returned her calls. He was sure Balyndah would report back to her she saw him at the game. Currently, it was tied up at fifty points apiece as the two teams headed into the halftime break.

"Is everything okay, Geno?" Sal asked. He noticed Geno seemed to be out of character and a tad bit distracted today. He observed him check his watch and his phone almost every fifteen minutes.

"Everything is all good, Sal. I was just waiting on a call. I left a ticket at the Will Call desk for someone to join us, but I guess he didn't show up," Geno replied.

"Who are you waiting for to show up?" Sal inquired curiously.

"It's not important. Let's go get some of this good food since its halftime," Geno suggested.

"That sounds like a plan," Cesare jumped in to state. He evidently was eavesdropping on their conversation.

Geno got up from his seat and headed over to the kitchen where the food was located. Sal and Cesare followed behind him. They all fixed a healthy plate of food and returned to their seats. While he ate his food, Geno's phone rang and it startled him. He almost dropped his plate when he attempted to answer the call. He put the phone to his ear and spoke a few words into the phone before he hung up. He put his plate down and walked over to where Cesare was standing talking to Milo. He tapped him on the shoulder to get his attention.

"Hey, Cesare, I need you to come take a walk with me," Geno stated.

"Take a walk to where? The second half is about to start and I don't want to miss seeing Westbrook and Wall go at it," Cesare responded.

"It's not a request. Let's go," Geno stated firmly. He had a serious look on his face. Cesare knew not to resist or question him any further. He followed behind him as they walked toward the door to exit. One of Geno's security guards tried to follow them, but Geno waved him off.

After they exited the suite, they were greeted by a cluster of people moving about the arena swiftly in an attempt to get back to their seats before the second half started. Geno and Cesare were headed in the opposite direction of the traffic toward the first level. When they reached the Will Call office, Geno saw who he was waiting for to arrive. Cesare was intrigued when he saw Geno shake hands with a tall, muscular African America man. He had never seen him before and was curious to know who he was for him to have to leave the game and come with Geno to meet him. He glanced in Cesare's direction as though he were sizing him up.

"I see you finally decided to show up, huh? I'm glad you could join us," Geno stated to the man in a joking manner.

"Yeah, I apologize for being late. I had a few things to take care of that held me up. So do you have good news for me?" the man asked.

"I said I would deliver for you, didn't I? The warrants have been quashed. That situation is a done deal," Geno replied.

"You are a man of your word. I can't thank you enough. Like I told you before, I owe you big time for this one and I pay my debts," Jericho stated to express his gratitude.

"Geno, who the hell is this guy? Can we get this over with so I can get back to the game?" Cesare asked angrily.

"Cesare, this right here is our brother, Jericho Jones. This is the son your father never told us about," Geno replied.

Cesare's jaw almost fell on the floor. Geno had told him about Jericho, but to meet him in person caught him off guard. As he glanced at him, he could see some of his father's facial features in Jericho.

"It's good to finally meet you. I can't believe this is real," Cesare uttered excitedly. He extended out his arm to shake Jericho's hand. Jericho returned the gesture.

"It's all good. I'm glad we got a chance to finally meet as well," Jericho stated.

"Don't mind him, Jericho, Cesare's a little short bus special," Geno joked. Jericho laughed as well.

"I don't know what to say right now, honestly," Jericho stated.

"There is nothing else for you to say. You're my guest tonight. I want you to meet a few of my trusted associates. Let's go enjoy the rest of the game in my suite. I'ma show you how I live and we can talk about a few things," Geno offered.

"Lead the way," Jericho stated accepting his invitation.

The three Caprese men made their way back up to the executive suite to join the rest of their party. They engaged in small talk. Cesare was amazed that he had another brother and that he was African American. He had always related to Black culture more than he did his own Italian heritage. He was also glad that they were around the same age because it was rough for him growing up with Geno and Silvio both being so much older than him.

The whole ride to the arena, Jericho was flustered by so many thoughts racing through his head. The conversation he recently had with Nina and Shavon was still fresh in his mind. He knew he would have to deal with them when he returned to the house and was unsure of how he would respond to their request. If he were to be honest with himself, he knew what they wanted from him was the right thing, but it was hard for him to break old habits, especially when he loved the art of the kill so much. Putting his feeling aside, he knew they depended on him and deserved better from him. Sooner or later he would have to make a decision to walk away from his lifestyle, but he expected for the day to come somewhere down the line at a later time.

In addition to that situation, he wondered what he would say to Geno when he saw him again. When Geno texted him and told him to meet him at the Wizards game, he accepted the offer strictly out of respect and gratitude for what Geno did for him. He wasn't a basketball fan at all. He rarely did public outings. His ability to be successful at what he did was rooted in his anonymity. Taking a break from his norm, Jericho decided to take a leap of faith and go against the grain. The fact that Geno was true to his word spoke volumes to Jericho. It meant he might be trustworthy and they might have a chance to develop a brotherly relationship.

When they finally reached the executive suite, everybody was focused on the game. The Wizards had a pulled ahead by a comfortable ten point margin headed into the fourth quarter. As they made their way up to where Geno was seated, all eyes turned toward Jericho. They all wondered who the stranger was that was with Geno and Cesare. Sal figured he must be a new business associate that Geno planned to introduce to announce another new venture he was considering embarking on. Geno decided to end the speculation.

"Can I get everybody's attention for just one minute? I know you're all wondering who the hell this guy is who just entered with me and Cesare. Well let me introduce you all to Jericho. He's our half-brother from another mother that I found out about not too long ago. Yeah, my old man was a low down dog, but hey, what can we do about that? Not a damn thing. Anyway, I want everybody to introduce themselves because Jericho is family now. He's a Caprese by blood and that's all that matters. He's one of us. You'll be seeing a lot more of him around if I have my way. Let's show him how we have a good time," Geno stated.

He was proud to have another younger brother to take under his wing. He saw potential in Jericho. He was cut from the same cloth as Geno in that they were both from the streets and lived by a strict code of loyalty and honor. If Jericho gave him a chance, he planned to open a new world of opportunity to him.

After the initial shock of his announcement wore off, everybody introduced themselves to Jericho one by one. Sal was a little upset because Geno failed to mention anything about Jericho before his announcement. He thought they were close like brothers, but after tonight he was unsure. As for Jericho, he was overwhelmed. For all of his life he had been a loner in search of a family. To be accepted so easily by Geno and his crew was a euphoric experience. Geno pulled him to the side so they could have a private conversation.

"Jericho, I know this all seems to be a bit much being as though we haven't really had a chance to get to know each other. However, I'm the kind of man that likes to go with his gut instinct. My gut tells me that you would be a perfect fit in my family. I know you make a lot of money freelancing doing hits with your partner, but I want to offer you a chance to do something different. I want to open a new world to you where you can make the same amount of money without having to worry about looking over your shoulder for the law. Hell, if the law comes looking for you and you're with my team, you already know you have nothing to worry about at all," Geno joked. Jericho had to laugh as well. Geno had already proven his worth to Jericho by what he did for him with his legal situation.

"So what did you have in mind? You have my attention," Jericho stated rather forthright. Thus far, Geno impressed him. He liked his confidence in his abilities. They both shared that same trait.

"I want to bring you on board at the Foundation and make you the head of my security team for starters. Like I said, you're family now and I take care of my own. You name your own salary and it's yours, but at least leave me enough money to buy food for the wife and kids," Geno joked.

"That's a tempting offer. I will have to consider it seriously," Jericho replied.

"Take a few days to think it over. When you decide what you want to do, let me know. That's enough of the serious talk. Go enjoy the rest of the game and all of this good food and liquor," he advised him. He decided to hold off on talking to Jericho about going to see Leonardo for now. He planned to bring it up at a later time if he decided to take him up on his offer.

Jericho took his advice. He helped himself to several plates of food and even had a few drinks. He and Cesare talked for a brief moment and made plans to get together at a later date. He looked forward to getting to know his new family better. He couldn't wait to tell Nina about Geno and Cesare. After the offer Geno just made, he might just have to consider Nina and Shavon's suggestion a little bit more seriously.

Chapter 19

It didn't take Elias long to settle into his new home after he was paid by Geno to leave Baltimore for good. In addition to the fifty grand he gave him, Geno arranged for him to have a new identity fully equipped with a fake birth certificate, social security number, and Maryland state identification card. His new name was Peter Simmons. It would take him a minute to adjust to the new name, but he didn't care. He was glad that Geno spared his life. He was also relieved he wouldn't have to worry about the police harassing him to try and get him to testify in court about what he saw the night Marcus was murdered.

His house in Baltimore was paid for in full. Before he left, he arranged to have the deed transferred into his son's name. He instructed him to sell the house and put the money he made from the sale in a trust fund for his grandchildren. It was the least he could do for them given the fact he wasn't an active part of their lives thus far. He also liquidated his retirement account and put the funds in a bank account under his new name. He decided to relocate to Queens, New York in the Flushing section. He figured it was easy to get lost in the mix in such a large city like New York.

Elias, or Peter, the name he would be called by from now on, found himself a spacious two bedroom apartment that was perfect. His landlord was a private owner which meant he didn't have to go through a background check to move in and could pay his rent in cash every month. His apartment was located in a quiet suburban area. His neighbors were friendly. Everybody generally minded their own business as they went about their day. He didn't need a car to get around the city because he could get to everywhere he needed to go by either cab, bus, or the train. He had a small neighborhood grocery store right on the corner where he went to buy food. There was a liquor store right across the street that he frequented to buy his daily dose of Tanqueray gin.

Even though he was in a new city under a new name, he still carried his old habits with him. It didn't him take him long to figure out where he the prostitutes were located. One of his neighbors told him about Roosevelt Avenue in the Jackson Heights area which was infamously known to be a haven for some of the finest young Latino hookers in the city. Elias became a regular in the area. He found a young pimp named, Pepe, who supplied him with as many girls as he desired as often as he liked. Even though he was a Baltimorean for almost his entire life, he had truly become comfortable as a New Yorker. This would be his home for the rest of his life if he had his way.

On this particular day, it was around noon when he finally woke up from another quiet night home where he just kicked back and watched movies on Netflix and sipped from his bottle of gin. He got up out of his bed to use the bathroom. After he washed his hands in the sink, he headed toward the kitchen to fix himself something to eat. When he looked in his refrigerator, he noticed he was out of eggs. He threw on a pair of jeans and a sweatshirt and headed out to the corner store to buy some more. He spoke to his next door neighbor, Louise, as he walked up the street. When he reached the corner store, he decided to buy a few extra items in addition to the dozen of eggs he originally planned to purchase. Once he got everything he needed, he headed back to his apartment.

"Elias! Elias Knox! Excuse me, can I speak with you for a minute?" a man yelled out from behind him.

When he heard someone call him by his birth name, it shook him up. He dropped the bag in his hand and his eggs splattered all over the concrete. When he turned around to see who it was, he almost fainted. He recognized the face of the person who called out his name. It was Detective Swift, the same police officer who questioned him about Marcus Harrison's murder. He shook his head and wondered what he did to have such bad luck. He thought he had left that situation behind him, but he was clearly wrong.

Elias made the mistake of using one of his old credit cards at the corner store several times to pay for his purchases. Detective Swift had been secretly tracking his financial transactions ever since the day he stopped by his house after Elias left Baltimore for good. When he got a hit several times on the same card from the same location, Swift decided to make a trip to New York, while he was off duty, to check out the lead. He sat out in front of the store for several days on a stakeout and hoped he ran across Elias or someone who could lead him to Elias. His instinct was dead on as today he hit the jackpot. When he saw Elias enter the store, he hopped out of his car and decided to approach him. He hoped he would finally get some answers to the questions that plagued his mind.

"You've got the wrong man. My name is Peter," Elias stated defiantly. At this point, he and Swift were almost face to face.

"Nice try, Mr. Knox. I know who you are and you know who I am. Can we go somewhere and talk for a minute?" Swift asked nicely.

"Talk about what? I have nothing to say to you. Isn't this out of your jurisdiction? Just leave me alone and go back to where you came from, man," Elias shouted at him.

"Look, we can do this the easy way or the hard way. You can talk to me now or I can go talk to the police here and get a warrant to have you brought into the police station so we can talk there. You know us boys in blue stick together," Swift stated. Elias was right about him having no jurisdiction in New York City, but he still decided to try his hand.

"Look, man I don't want no trouble. I'm sorry that boy got killed. It's a tragedy, but I didn't kill him. Stop harassing me," Elias pleaded with him. He wished he had kept his mouth shut that night.

"If you tell me what I want to know, you can go on about your business. Judging by the fact you sold your house and moved here out of the blue, it's clear to me that either you were paid off to leave or you left because you were scared. Which one is it?" Swift asked.

"Look man, I don't want any problems. If I tell you anything, those people will kill me. I'm just an old man trying to live out my final days in peace," Elias uttered.

"What people? Who is going to kill you? I can protect you if you feel your life's in danger," Swift offered.

"I'm talking about that big time lawyer guy. He owns all of those businesses too. He's on all of those billboards all over the city. His goons kidnapped me from my house one day and told me to keep my mouth shut about that murder or they would kill me," Elias stated. He figured there wasn't any point lying anymore because Swift wouldn't go away. If Swift found him in New York, he wouldn't rest until he got the answers he wanted.

"Are you talking about Geno Caprese?" he asked. Swift's mind was blown. He couldn't believe what he just heard. He had to be mistaken.

"Yeah, that's the one. He paid me to leave town and even gave me a new identity," Elias stated.

"I need you to come with me," Swift instructed him.

"I'm not going anywhere with you. I'm not under arrest. This isn't Baltimore City. You're just a regular citizen here. You can't do anything to me. I can call the police and have you arrested for harassing me. You got what you wanted now would you please leave me alone," Elias barked at him as he walked away.

"You're right I don't have any jurisdiction here. I'm just trying to do the right thing. An innocent man is in jail now for this murder while the real killer is still free. Here's my card. Please call me if you need my help for anything. I will definitely be in touch very soon," Swift promised him as he walked away. Elias had no intention of calling him. In fact, he was on his way to pack his things and get out of town as fast as he could.

He had to take a moment to catch his breath and process what Elias just told him. He knew there was something different about this case, but he didn't expect to hear Geno Caprese was involved. He remembered his brief interaction with him when he questioned his brother Cesare about the murder of his girlfriend a while back. This could be a huge, career defining moment to be able to tie Geno to criminal activity after law enforcement failed to nail him for anything for so many years. He jumped in his car and headed back to Baltimore. This case just took on a new life.

Chapter 20

It took Jericho a few days to finally make up his mind about the opportunity he was presented with by Geno. He had a lot of things to consider before he gave him an answer. Even though Geno's offer was extremely generous and could provide him with a chance to do something different with his life, he had to reconcile with himself the fact he would have to walk away from the only lifestyle he knew. He never had a regular job before and wasn't accustomed to operating in a structured environment. Even though he got his client assignments from Gutta, he had total autonomy to work on his own terms in planning out every contract killing he fulfilled. If he accepted Geno's offer, he would be working for him and have to answer to him. He wasn't sure his ego could handle not being in total control regardless of how much money he was paid.

To help him make a decision about the offer, Jericho talked it over with Shavon and Nina. In doing so, he had to go into detail about who Geno was and how he helped them get out of their legal situation. He told her about their other brother, Cesare, as well. He told her how he thought they were stand up men and appeared to be genuinely interested in developing a relationship with them. He also told her their father, Leonardo, was dying from cancer. When Shavon found out Jericho actually had a chance to meet their long lost brothers, she initially had mixed emotions. She knew who Geno was because when she worked as a paralegal, the attorney she worked for, Gregory Adams, spoke highly of him. Attorney Adams considered Geno to be one of the best attorneys he had ever had the privilege of litigating against in the courtroom.

She was intrigued and curious enough to want to meet him because she wanted to pick his brain for some of his legal expertise that could help with her future plans. She intended to return to school to pursue a law degree once she was fully back on her feet. She was also hesitant about meeting him because for so long it had just been her and Jericho. She had developed a comfort zone with them being the only family each other had. She wasn't sure she wanted to share her brother with anyone else just yet. As for the news about their father, she fought back the desire to want to continue hating him for not being there for them for so long. She told

Jericho she wanted to go see him before he died because it would help her make peace with their past. She told him he needed to do the same because it was time for them both to let go of the hurt and disappointment they both carried around for so long.

Nina was excited to know Jericho had reconnected with his siblings. After he told her about the job offer, she viewed it as a blessing in disguise. In her eyes, it was the perfect chance for him to try his hand at something new. Even though Geno was still involved with criminal activity and he still faced some degree of danger working as his head of security, she was optimistic about Jericho's chances of moving around in Geno's organization to be able work toward transitioning into a position in one of his legal business ventures. She had reached a point in their relationship where she was tired of worrying about Jericho every time he left out for a new assignment. She simply wanted him to do something different. Lately, the thought crossed her mind a lot that it was time for them to start a family soon. She wanted to have Jericho's children. She was sure he would be a good father because his experience not having one would make him want to do everything necessary not to disappoint his own children.

After his discussions with both Shavon and Nina, Jericho took a few days to himself to process it all. They gave him a lot of things to consider before he made a decision not just about the job offer, but his life in general. For so long he had operated off of his hatred of Leonardo and the pain from his mother's death, that he began to think it was time for him to do some soul searching to discover who he really was as a man. He needed to gain a deeper understanding of himself as a person. He wondered if the only legacy he wanted to leave the world was a long list of dead bodies. When Nina mentioned the possibility of them having children one day, he began to realize he had to make some changes in his life. He couldn't continue to live such a dangerous lifestyle that could place his children in harm's way because of his actions. He also didn't want his children to grow up without him because he knew the impact it would have on them based on his own personal experience.

His conversations with Nina and Shavon, as well as his own moments of reflection about his life, played a part in his decision to take a leap of faith and take Geno up on his offer. He knew Gutta would be upset when he told him the news, but he would eventually get over it and move on with conducting business as usual. Jericho had to do what was best for him and the family he hoped to have one day with Nina. Shavon also forced him to accept that it was time for them to finally confront their negative feelings toward their father head on. That was why he was on his way to the hospice facility now to see him. Shavon and Nina came along with him. Geno and Cesare agreed to meet them there as well. The time had come for all of Leonardo's children to deal with the demons that had plagued them as a result of his actions.

When they arrived at the facility, Jericho noticed Geno's car parked out front. He parked his car in an open spot and walked toward the vehicle. Geno and Cesare stepped out of the vehicle when they saw the three of them coming in their direction. When they were within arm's reach of each other, Jericho introduced everybody. This was the first time Shavon had been out publicly since her brutal rape. She had some anxiety, but that quickly faded because Nina was by her side for support. She embraced both Geno and Cesare in a tight clinch. She was happy to meet them. She had no ill will toward them because of Leonardo. They were happy to meet her as well. This family reunion was long overdue.

"Are you all ready for this? I know I'm not," Geno stated honestly.

"I'm as ready as I'll ever be," Jericho chimed in.

"I want to see him because I have a few things on my mind to say that I think he needs to hear," Shavon stated passionately.

"I can agree with you there, Shavon," Geno stated as they made toward the hospice facility.

Geno opened the door so Shavon could enter first. They all followed closely behind her as they made their way inside of the facility. They stopped at the front desk. Geno asked for Leonardo's room number from the person at the front desk. She gave him the information and they headed toward the elevator. The ride to the floor Leonard was on seemed like an eternity. When the elevator doors opened, it was time to face the music.

They all stepped off the elevator and headed toward Leonardo's room. Geno called his mother beforehand to let her know they would all be coming to visit their father. It was a bittersweet moment for Marietta as well. To finally lay eyes on her husband's other children would give her a chance to confront the negative feelings she harbored toward them as well because it wasn't their fault Leonardo cheated on her with their mother. She was also happy she was able to make Leonardo's final wish to see all of his children one last time come to pass.

When they reached Leonardo's room, Geno entered first by himself. His mother was seated by his father's bed in the room all alone. Leonardo was propped up on his pillows. He had lost a lot of weight since the last time Geno saw him and his complexion was very pale. Even though he was in bad shape physically, his lively spirit was still there as he joked around with Marietta. When Leonardo turned around and saw Geno standing in the doorway, a big smile came across his face. Marietta was happy to see him as well. She got up and gave him a big hug. She then walked out of the room so they could have a moment alone.

"There he is! That's my son. Get over here! You don't know how much I've missed you!" Leonardo declared loudly with tears in his eyes.

This was the first time Geno ever saw his father cry. He walked toward him and did his best to fight his urge to shed tears as well, but he couldn't help himself. When he embraced Leonardo, he hugged him as tight as he could without hurting his frail frame. To see him in such a weak state and to know he wouldn't be around much longer made Geno feel like a fool for holding a grudge against a man who had done so much for him.

"Pops, I missed you too. It's hard for me see you like this. I'm sorry for how I've been acting. I was wrong! I was wrong!" Geno repeated over and over as he was overcome with a burst of emotions.

"You have nothing to apologize for, son. This is my burden to bear. I always told you and your brothers a real man takes responsibility for his own actions. I messed up and let you all down and for that I'm sorry. I made a big mess of so many lives," Leonardo stated. He made an honest assessment of his misdeeds from the past.

"So, how are you feeling?" Geno asked attempting to lighten up the mood in the room.

"I'm hanging on. It hurts everywhere. I'm in pain all day and night. They tell me I can go any day now, but I tell them to go to hell. I survived out in these streets for so many years that fighting this cancer thing is a piece of cake. Plus, I told the man upstairs he can't have me until I see all of my children," Leonardo joked. Geno had to smile at his father's resilient spirit in the face of his dire medical condition.

"I have something to tell you about Silvio, Pops. Let's just say he didn't stay true to this thing of ours and is no longer with us," Geno confessed. He knew his father understood exactly what he meant by his statement. He was the one who taught him the laws of the streets and the consequences for those who betrayed the code. Leonardo paused for a moment and took a deep breath before he spoke.

"I know you did what you had to do, son. Silvio was always jealous of you ever since you were born. God bless his soul. I always told you that if you live this life of ours there would come a day you would have to make a choice to do some things you didn't want to do, but had to do if you wanted to survive. I guess my words of wisdom came to pass," Leonardo stated. Geno nodded his head in agreement.

"I do have a surprise for you that I know you will like. I'll be right back."

Geno got up from the edge of the bed and walked out of the room. He returned a shortly thereafter with Cesare, Jericho, and Shavon. When he saw them all enter the room, the moment was surreal. No words could capture the euphoria that overcame him. To see all of his children together was a dream come true. This was a moment he dreamed about for years, but one he didn't have the courage to make happen because of his own shortcomings. Shavon remained in the lobby because she wanted Jericho and Nina to share this time with their father. Marietta stood in the doorway and remained a silent observer. How she felt didn't matter right now. This was Leonardo's moment.

"Wow, let me see you all. I can't believe this! Is this Jericho? I see you got my good looks. Is this Shavon? You look just like your mother," Leonardo stated. He couldn't believe his eyes. He swore he had died and gone to heaven. He couldn't believe they came to see him. He reached out his arms to them. Shavon stepped forward and grabbed his hand. A rush of emotions ran through her body. Geno grabbed his other hand and shook it firmly.

"Do you know how long we both hated you for not being there for us? You were our father! We needed you! We needed you!" she yelled at him. Jericho wrapped his arms around her to console her.

"I am sorry, Shavon. I am sorry, Jericho. I don't know what else to say. I don't know what else to do. You should hate me. You have every right to feel that way about me. I wasn't a father to you at all. Cesare I treated you wrong too. I'm sorry. Will you all please forgive me?" he asked. There was a deafening silence in the room. He awaited their response.

"I forgive you. I can't forget what you did or should I say didn't do, but I forgive you," Jericho stated boldly. His response caught them all by surprise. It was big step for him to make. Shavon looked at him with pride.

"Thank you, son, I know I don't deserve forgiveness, but I thank you anyway," Leonardo replied humbly.

For the next hour or so, they engaged in conversation with no ill words being exchanged. This wasn't the time or place for those feelings to surface. It was a time for healing for them all. Leonardo was able to get his last wish to see all of his children so he could make amends with them. This was a moment that was long overdue yet still necessary.

They all had no clue that their family reunion was being observed by Detective Swift. He had been tailing Geno ever since his run-in with Elias in New York City. He was trying to make a connection between Geno, Jericho, Shavon, and Nina so he could have enough information to submit to his superiors to reopen Marcus' case. After what he just witnessed today, the connection started to become clearer.

As for Leonardo, sadly he passed away three days later in his sleep. Shavon and Jericho regretted not having more time to spend with him, but they knew that was out of their hands to control. His funeral was a festive occasion. There were over two thousand people in attendance to celebrate his life. There were gangsters, politicians, actors, actresses, and a host of others from all walks of life who came to pay their respects to him. Geno made sure he had the most expensive and stylish casket the funeral parlor had because his father deserved the best. He had the phrase "Here lies a Gangster, Gentleman, and Father" etched into his headstone. As flawed as he was as a person, he also made a positive impact on the lives of many and deserved to be remembered favorably.

Chapter 21

Sal was home alone in his comfortable three bedroom single family house located in Reisterstown, Maryland. He was unwinding after another long day of work. He was so tired that he collapsed on the couch in his living room and didn't even bother to take off his shoes. He grabbed his remote control and turned on the television to find something to watch. He couldn't find anything that caught his eye so he turned the television off and decided to pick up where he left off with the latest Clive Cussler novel he had started reading. He was a big fan of the author and owned his entire collection. Reading was one of his favorite leisure activities on the rare occasion that he had some free time.

Lately, Geno upped Sal's workload so much that, at times, he felt overwhelmed. He didn't

complain to Geno about his added duties because
Geno also increased his salary to reflect the change.
Plus, he also knew that if he did complain, there
was a chance Geno would lessen his role at the
Foundation and give the assignments to someone
else. It was clear to him that Geno had a plan in
motion to move Cesare up the ranks to position him
by his side in a leadership position. In addition to
what he had in store for Cesare, it was also obvious
that Geno would eventually make room for his long
lost brother, Jericho, to join him in running the
Foundation. Sal observed all of Geno's maneuvers
astutely. He knew he had to stay on his A game if
he wanted to maintain his position as Geno's right
hand man. He felt as though he deserved
everything he got because he put in the work and
remained loyal to Geno from the time the
Foundation was just an idea up until it was the
business powerhouse it had now become. He
planned to do all he could to remind Geno of his
value to the corporation.

Before he knew it, almost two hours had passed
since he got home. He decided it was time for him
to get up off of the couch when his growling
stomach reminded him that he needed to eat. He
glanced at his watch and was surprised to see that
it was almost nine o'clock in the evening. Sal got up
from the couch and made his way into the kitchen
to find something to eat. When he looked in his
refrigerator, he saw the plate of spaghetti he had
left over from the other night and decided that

would be his meal for the night. He popped the plate in the microwave for three minutes to heat up. While he waited, he poured himself a glass of wine. Once his food was ready, he sat down at his kitchen table to devour the plate. When he was done, he headed toward his bedroom to take a shower. He was usually in bed by ten because he liked to be well rested when he went into the office in the morning.

While he was in the shower, Sal was startled by what he thought sounded like glass shattering somewhere in his the downstairs area of his home. Instinctively, he hopped out of the shower, grabbed his towel to dry off and he reached for his cell phone, which was on the sink. He had security cameras installed throughout his house that he could monitor from his phone. When he pulled the cameras up on his phone, he was surprised to see two masked men moving about his living room area. He quickly grabbed his boxer briefs off the floor and threw on a pair of shorts. He made his way into his bedroom and grabbed the loaded 9 mm handgun he slept with under his pillow every night. He carefully made his way out of his bedroom into the hallway area with his phone in one hand and his gun in the other one. He saw the men headed toward the stairs to make their way up to the upper level of the house. He made a mad dash to beat them to the punch. When he reached the steps, one of the men was halfway up the stairs.

"I got your ass motherfucker!" Sal yelled as he squeezed the trigger on his gun.

He nailed his target twice in the chest area. The intruder fell backward up against the wall. His blood splattered everywhere. When he saw his partner was hit, the other intruder let off several shots from his gun as he retreated in the opposite direction. Sal let off several more shots as he advanced forward. He stepped over the intruder he shot because he assumed he was dead. When he reached the downstairs area, he saw the other man make a mad dash across his lawn and hop into a dark colored car. He sped off as he made his escape. Sal, out of breath, walked back toward the stairs in the direction of the man he had shot. He was surprised to see him crawling down the stairs in his direction.

"Please, don't kill me!" the man pleaded.

"Take off your mask, you son of a bitch! Show your face!" Sal barked at him.

The wounded intruder did as he was instructed. He raised his hands in the air in an attempt to surrender.

"I'll tell you whatever you want to know. Please don't kill me!"

"Who sent you, motherfucker? Who do you work for?" Sal asked with his gun pointed at him.

"Rah sent sent me! I work for Rah! He sent me to kill you as revenge for what you did to his father, Nesta! He plans to kill you and the rest of your crew that were responsible for his death. I told you what you wanted to know now can you call an ambulance for me? I don't want to die! Please don't kill me!" he begged. Blood poured from his wounds.

"Thanks for the information," Sal said before he squeezed the trigger three more times to put him out of his misery.

Sal was pressed for time because he was sure his neighbors would call the police after hearing the gunshots. He needed to get a cleanup crew in quickly to get rid of the body and any evidence of the shooting. He placed a call to someone who could take care of the job. After that was done, he called Geno. He answered on the second ring.

"Hey, Sal what's up?" he asked.

"Geno, we have a problem," he replied. He ran down the details of what just went down to him. Geno was heated.

"After they finish cleaning up, you need to get the hell out of there. I'll call you in a few. Me and Clay will meet you somewhere so we can decide our next move," Geno instructed him before he hung up. They had a serious problem on their hands. Rah was clearly out for blood to avenge his father's death. It was clear he had a plan already set in motion. If Rah wanted a war that was exactly what they planned to give him.

Chapter 22

Urban Gear Central was one of the most profitable stores located in White Marsh Mall. The store sold all of the hottest designer clothing brands worn by the younger generation today, both male and female. The affordable prices made the store so popular. They had something for everybody. It appealed to the preppy college student, young professional worker, and flashy drug dealer all at the same time. They all came there to shop for a hot outfit to wear to school, work, or out to the club. There were clothing sizes to fit any body type from petite to plump to big and tall. If you left out empty handed, it either meant you were a window shopper or you had no fashion sense at all.

The store stayed busy with a steady flow of traffic, with the busiest days being on the weekends. The amount of revenue generated made the store owners, Milton and Jarvis Jackson, very happy men. It was the first legitimate business they opened many years ago and it was still a profitable venture for them today. To have staying power in the retail business was a difficult thing for many local business owners to do in the current economy. They saw many of their local competitors go out of business because they were unable to hold on to their customer base for whatever reason. The fact they were able to still have loyal customers for such a long period of time was a testament to their clever marketing and advertising techniques. They were currently considering opening two additional locations in two other malls in the city to further expand their brand.

It was almost closing time and Pauletta, the store manager, was hard at work straightening up the misplaced clothes on the shelves and racks. Even though it was almost nine o'clock in the evening, there were still a few customers browsing around the store in attempt to do some last minute shopping. She stopped what she was doing briefly to glance at her watch and just shook her head from side to side. She wished they would all hurry up and decide what they wanted to purchase so she could ring up their orders and close out her drawer for the night. She really didn't want to be at work today, but had no choice but to be there because Isis, the sales associate who was scheduled to work tonight, called out sick and she didn't have time to find another employee to fill in for her. Jarvis, who also happened to be her long-time boyfriend, made it mandatory for her as the manager to step up and work in such unforeseen situations. Pauletta really couldn't complain because he paid her almost six figures per year, which was an excellent salary for someone with just a high school diploma.

Pauletta had finished straightening up the clothes and was on her way over to the shoe racks when she noticed one of the customers walking toward the cash register with two hands full of clothing, which indicated he was ready to check out. The other two customers who were walking around the store made their way toward the door to exit out into the mall without making a purchase. They obviously fit in the window shopper category. Once she rung up her final customer's items, her work day was a wrap. She could finally head home to get some much needed rest only to have to be back at work bright and early in the morning to do it all over again.

"Your total will be four hundred and thirty-two dollars and seventy-six cents, Sir. Will that be cash, debit, or charge?" she asked him.

He was a well built man with a midnight black shaded skin tone who looked to be in his early twenties. He had dreadlocks which hung down past his shoulders onto his chest area. His emerald green eyes caught her attention because it was rare to find a Black man his complexion who had eyes that color.

"Sweetheart, do you know who I am? I'm Johnny Blaze. I only pay cash for everything I want. Credit is for those fools who can't afford to pay for what they want up front, you feel me?" he asked.

Johnny Blaze reached in his pocket and peeled off five crisp one hundred dollar bills out of his rubber band full of money to pay her. She gladly took his money out of his hand, put it in the register, and gave him his change along with the receipt. She couldn't wait for him to be on his way and out of her face. She hated when a man tried to floss in front of her because it showed a lack of class.

"Thank you for your business, and please come again. I hope you enjoy the rest of your evening," she said in her most professional voice.

"I would enjoy it even more if your let me take you out to dinner tonight. Me and you cruising in my Ghost would be a good look. What time do you get off?" he asked with a big grin on his face. He was used to females being impressed when he mentioned what kind of car he drove, but little did he know Pauletta drove a Bentley Continental of her own.

"I appreciate the offer, but my man wouldn't like that too much," she replied as respectfully as she could. Even though he was a cocky asshole she saw no reason for her to stoop to his level.

"Well, what your man doesn't know won't hurt him. I won't tell him if you won't," he shot back at her. He got bold and leaned up against the counter in an attempt to put his best mack game down. Pauletta wasn't the least bit impressed. In fact, she laughed in his face.

"You won't have to tell him because he heard you ask me out on a date. He's standing right behind you," she replied bluntly. She motioned with her hand for him to turn around.

Johnny Blaze almost jumped out of his skin and had a heart attack when he saw Jarvis standing right behind him with a serious look on his face like he was ready to bash in his skull. Jarvis wasn't really upset because Pauletta handled herself properly when she turned him down politely. He was secure in his relationship and had no reason to worry about a peon like Johnny Blaze taking his woman.

"Awww, man, I know who you are! You're one of the Jackson brothers! I owe you an apology. I didn't know this was your lady, Sir. This was just a misunderstanding," he stated in an attempt to cop a plea. He recognized Jarvis' face and instantly realized he had made a big mistake pushing up on Pauletta. Every young hustler in the city knew of the Jackson brothers and their notorious reputation in the streets. They all aspired to become OG's in the drug game like they did. Johnny Blaze did his best to try and save face without making even more of a jackass of himself.

"It's all good, young blood. There's no harm done. You saw a pretty face and tried your hand. I would've done the same thing. Enjoy the rest of your night, young soldier," Jarvis uttered as he patted Johnny Blaze on the shoulder and sent him on his way. He exited the store in a hurry. Jarvis closed the gate behind him to lock up for the night.

"So, you would've done the same thing if you walked in a store and saw a pretty face? Is that what you do when I'm not around?" she asked him. She had come from behind the counter and stood in front of the cash register with her hands on her shapely hips.

"Baby, the only pretty face I'm interested in is yours, sweet thang," he replied. He walked toward her and grabbed her into his arms. He kissed her flush in the mouth to let her know she was his one and only. He came to the store every night at closing so he could accompany her when she dropped the day's cash proceeds off at the bank.

"Yeah, it better be or else I'ma have to hurt somebody," she replied playfully. She broke free from his grasp and walked back behind the counter to remove the cash drawer from the register so she could take it into the back office and tally up all of the day's earnings. Jarvis followed closely behind her while he playfully patted her on her rear end several times.

Jarvis and Pauletta had been a couple for almost seven years. In fact, their seventh year anniversary was coming up on the seventeenth of next month. Jarvis planned to surprise her by whisking her away for a week long romantic getaway to the Virgin Islands to celebrate. He recently purchased a stunning five carat platinum diamond engagement ring for Pauletta. He intended to finally propose to her while they were on their trip. He had an elaborate plan laid out to make it a magical moment. He rented out one of the most exquisite restaurants on the island for the evening for them to have a quiet, romantic dinner all alone. He hired a local band to play jazz music all night and had a singer who would serenade her when he asked for her hand in marriage. With all of the effort he put into the proposal, there was no way she could turn him down. Outside of the fact he loved her, she had put up with him for seven years and remained rock solid the entire time to prove her loyalty and devotion to him. It was only right he finally made an honest woman of her.

While Pauletta sat behind the desk and added up the money, Jarvis sat across from her surfing the web on his cell phone. He took a brief break from his phone to glance up at her to admire how beautiful she was. He was totally captivated by her smooth, dark skin and full lips. She kept her hair cut in a short style which made her face stand out. She had a small, shapely frame which suited Jarvis just fine because he liked his women petite.

"Baby, we had an awesome day today. It didn't seem like we made this much money because the store traffic seemed slower than usual, but I guess I was wrong," Pauletta stated. Jarvis was happy as well because the more money the store made, the more money he and Milton made to increase their wealth. She placed all of the cash inside of the bag they planned to drop off at the bank.

"That's how it is sometimes, Pauletta. It's not always about how many people come in the store, but it's about how much money the people who do come to shop spend. You can have a few people spend more money buying a gang of stuff while a larger number of people just buy one item. Either way you look at it, sweetie, I'm proud of you. I think you need to take a few days off to relax. You deserve a little break. Let Shakima run the store for you," he suggested.

Shakima was the assistant manager at the store. She was a young college student and Pauletta's cousin. She hired her to work at the store so she could make money to pay for school. She was a smart girl and a fast learner. She fit in well at the store.

"That sounds like a good idea, baby. I think I'm going to take the next few days and just relax," Pauletta stated. A few days off would suit her just fine. Her feet ached from being on them all day. Her back and shoulders were sore as well from lifting boxes and keeping the racks and shelves adequately stocked with clothing.

"It's getting late. Let's get out of here," Jarvis uttered after he looked at his watch to check the time.

"I'm ready. Let me just grab my purse and my keys and we can go," Pauletta stated.

She got up to retrieve the items while Jarvis grabbed the bag of money. Even though Milton always told him to bring security with him for protection when he made the money drop, Jarvis felt it was unnecessary. The shiny black revolver he had tucked in his dip was all the security he felt he needed. Jarvis unlocked the gate and lifted it up so they could exit the store. He locked it back behind him. They waved to the mall security guards as they walked out of the mall. It took them a few minutes to stroll through the parking lot before they found Jarvis' truck. He opened up Pauletta's door and helped her get inside of the truck. As he walked over to the other side to hop in the driver's seat, he heard the screeching sound of car tires behind him. When he turned around, he saw a Black Cadillac with pitch black tinted windows blocking his truck in.

Before he had a chance to reach for his gun, two young black men jumped out of the car with their guns drawn. They had the drop on him. Jarvis simply threw his hands in the air to surrender. The gunman on the passenger side inched closer to him and pointed his guns directly at his face. The other gunman came around from the driver's side and stood next to his partner. Pauletta heard the screeching sound of the car's tires and glanced in the mirror to see what was going down. When she saw the two men with their guns pointed at Jarvis, her heart sunk in her chest, but she didn't panic. She knew Jarvis kept a gun in a secret compartment he had built on the passenger door. He took her to the gun range on a regular so she was a pretty good shot. Pauletta reached inside of the compartment and pulled out the .38 revolver Jarvis kept inside for added protection. She watched the interaction between Jarvis and the two gun men and positioned herself to hop out of the car at the right moment. She planned to jump out firing. Scared or not, she would do whatever was necessary to defend her man.

"Make a wrong move and I'll blow your head off!" one of the men threatened. As he glanced closely at him, Jarvis recognized his face. It was Johnny Blaze, the same young man who was just in the store flirting with Pauletta.

"Is that why you were flirting with my lady, lil' homey? You were watching my store to set me up to rob me? Just take the money. You can have it all, but you're making a big mistake right now. You must not really know who I am. You have no idea what you just did, do you? You both just committed suicide," Jarvis stated as he chuckled.

"No, I was flirting with your lady because she's got a nice body and I wanted to hit that thing from behind. Yeah, I've been watching you for a minute leading up to this moment. I know exactly who you are Jarvis Jackson. This ain't about the money, but we will take that too. This is payback for what you and crew did to Nesta, motherfucker!" the young man yelled before he let off several rounds.

Jarvis fell to the ground and grabbed his chest. Jarvis' hands were soaked in his own blood as he gasped for air. The bag of money fell down next to him. The other gunman grabbed the bag and turned around to walk back toward the car. After she heard the gunshots and saw Jarvis fall to the ground, out of sheer instinct, Pauletta hopped out of the truck and started firing off rounds from the in the direction of Johnny Blaze and his accomplice. She wasn't concerned about her life at this point. The two robbers made a mad dash back to their car while they dodged bullets. One of the bullets hit Johnny Blaze because he grabbed his shoulder and yelled out in pain as he hopped in the passenger seat. The driver put the pedal to the metal and sped off. The loud screeching sound of the tires echoed loudly in the parking lot when they exited the scene. When they were gone, Pauletta ran back to the truck and grabbed her cell phone to call 911. Then, she raced over to where Jarvis was and saw him lying in a pool of his blood clutching his chest. She got down on the ground and held him in her arms. Blood flowed from his chest freely.

"Them bastard got me! It was Nesta's people that shot me! Call my brother! Call Geno! We've got to strike back hard and fast at these bastards to remind them who we are and what we do!" he uttered valiantly. Even as he clung on for dear life, Jarvis was a street soldier at heart ready to do battle with his enemies. However, to Pauletta, he was her man. He was her rock and foundation. To see him dying right before her eyes was traumatic, but she did her best to remain positive for him.

"Okay, baby, I'll call them in a minute. For now, I just need you to hold on for me until the ambulance gets here," Pauletta stated as calmly as she could given the circumstances. She rocked him back and forth in her arms. His eyes open and shut several times. His breathing became shallow. Pauletta was covered in her tears and his blood. She breathed a sigh of relief when she heard the sounds of sirens getting closer and closer to where they were located.

Chapter 23

It was almost one o'clock in the morning and the crowd had begun to thin out at Lila's. The DJ just shouted over the microphone there was only one hour left for everybody to order their last rounds of drinks. There were three girls up on the stage bouncing up and down to the music. They were working hard in an effort to get the few customers still there to tip them with all of the remaining one dollar bills they had left in their hands. The girls lived for nights like tonight when the men would come into Lila's and drink round after round from the bar. The drunker they were, the looser they were with their money. That meant more tips for the girls who worked hard as they could to entice the men with their naughty body movements. It was something about the combination of naked women, alcohol, and loud, thumping bass music which could drive even the most square and straight laced man to exercise bad judgment by spending all of his hard earned money just for a chance to dry hump a stripper in the VIP section of the bar.

One of the girls on stage, Raven, was more thirsty than the other two. She was a hustler and determined to claim every dollar she could from the young drug dealers or working men who were mesmerized by all of the flexible positions she could twist her body into while dancing on the pole. She was extremely agile for a woman with such a thick figure. Even though she was new to Lila's, Raven was one of the biggest money makers in the club. She would go the extra mile to do all of the freaky things the other girls wouldn't do to make sure she went home with enough money to meet the goal she set for herself every night she worked. She had two children to take care of alone along with a sick father who suffered from lupus. She had a lot of expensive financial obligations to pay on her own. Raven truly defined the concept of using what you got to get what you want. The Creator blessed her with a beautiful body and she used every bit of it to her advantage to get ahead in life. She was a go-getter in every sense of the phrase.

While she danced for her final song, the other two girls up on the stage stopped and looked at her with envy when she plopped down in front of Moreno and did a split. She showed him how flexible she was when stretched out her legs and wrapped them around his neck. She pulled his face toward her and buried his head in her crotch. Moreno didn't mind one bit. He inhaled the scent of her sweaty perfume while he enjoyed the up close and personal view of her private parts. The other girls were jealous because they were working hard to be as raunchy as could be, but all of the guys had their full attention on Raven. To see her forty eight inch butt and slender waist move about the stage was breathtaking.

"Damn, girl, your body is banging! I'm trying to get with you tonight after the club closes!" Moreno barked at her over the loud music. He reached in his pocket and pulled out a knot of cash so fast it almost popped the rubber band it was wrapped in.

"Is all of that money for me?" she asked when she bent off the stage down and whispered in his ear. He nodded his head to give an affirmative response.

Meanwhile, Raven made her way back to center stage to finish out her routine. She bent over and hoisted her butt up in the air for all of the men to see and admire. It jiggled every time she playfully spanked herself. The men all broke their necks in a race against each other to see her shake it up close and personal. Moreno paid them all no mind when he got up from his seat and made his way through the crowd and smacked her on the butt with the pile of one dollar bills in his hand. Raven didn't mind when customers touched her as long as they tipped well. That was never a problem for Moreno and his boys, Che and Kurt. It was nothing for them to drop ten or twenty thousand dollars in a night just to watch Raven and the rest of the ladies dirty dance and get naked. They paid extra to see some girl on girl action pop off on stage. The money they spent at Lila's was a drop in the bucket compared to how much they made every week selling drugs for Milton and Jarvis. Whenever they dropped a few stacks of cash frivolously, it just motivated them to grind harder out in the streets to make even more.

"Raven, if you ride this big python in my pants right, you can have whatever you want from me. Let's get up out of here and go back to my house," Moreno pleaded with her.

He drank close to a fifth of Hennessy and a few shots of Patron over the course of a few hours. He was drunk out of his mind and horny as ever. He grabbed his crotch and just imagined what he could do with Raven in the bed if she gave him a chance. He had his eye on her for a minute. Raven turned down guys every night who offered her big money to go home with them at the end of her shift. However, Moreno was more determined than most. That was why he normally got whatever girl he wanted. He would go the extra mile and say and do whatever was necessary to get between a woman's thighs. To have bragging rights about being the first one to have sex with Raven would do wonders for his ego. He had it in his mind that tonight was the night it would all go down.

"You ain't said nothing but a word, player. I hope you're ready for this right here," she teased him.

Raven thought Moreno was attractive as well. She also thought his money was even more attractive. She had a thing for thugged out dudes with money who loved to spoil her. Moreno clearly fit the mold. The fact he was part of the Jackson brothers inner circle made him even more appealing. His persistence let her know he was pressed to get with her. Tonight she planned to give in to him. She wanted to see if he could really do all of the things he claimed he could to her body.

Raven finished up her set and proceeded to walk toward the steps at the end of the stage. Moreno's eyes locked in on her thick calves. The nine inch heels she had on made her calf muscles look even more defined. Raven was five feet and six inches of pure sexiness that he wanted to sink his teeth in. He reached out his hand to help her walk down the steps. His boys, Che and Kurt, busted out laughing at him. They were amused because they rarely saw Moreno act this way over a woman. Girls usually chased and stalked him and not the other way around. Just as he was about to walk with her back over to his seat, one of the security guards tapped him on the shoulder.

"Milton wants to see you," he yelled into his ear because the music in the club was so loud.

"He picked one hell of a time to want to see me," Milton mumbled under his breath.

Moreno was pissed as hell. His member was rock hard and he had nothing but having sex on his mind at the moment. He wondered what Milton wanted with him right now. He was confident he was about to leave the club with Raven, but instead he had to go and meet up with Milton. He always talked his head off in an attempt to impart his wisdom onto him. He preached to him about not spending so much of his money frivolously on strippers and alcohol. Milton was like Geno in this respect. He wanted Moreno to become a smart businessman who made it out of the hood to become another success story. However, Moreno just wanted to run the streets and earn his money in the trap.

Moreno remembered how all of his so called friends in the music industry turned their backs on him after he lost his voice and couldn't sing anymore, but his homeboys he grew up with remained solid and by his side. The hood was his comfort zone and he never planned to leave it behind. In spite of his resistance to change, Milton still persisted with his efforts.

Reluctantly, Moreno walked back to Milton's office. When he reached his office, he walked in.

Milton was seated behind his desk with his feet up reading over some paperwork.

"Milton, what's up man? I was just about to step off for the night with that fine ass Raven. What do you need from me?" Moreno asked.

"There you go again always thinking with your little head in your pants and not the big one on your head. Have a seat for a minute," he instructed him.

Moreno took a seat across from him with his arms folded. He was heated because the only thing he loved more than money was a nice, firm ass like the one Raven had. Nothing stood in his way when he was ready to get his freak on. He got tunnel vision when it came to getting laid.

"So, what's good, cuz?" Moreno asked.

"I just wanted to properly thank you for what you did for us with the situation with your man Sticky. Getting him to take that charge was greatly appreciated by the big man," Milton stated in reference to Geno.

"Oh, that was easy work. That fool owed me five stacks and I told him I would forgive his debt if he took the charge. At first, he turned me down, but then he saw the light when I told him I was going to kill his mother and his whole family. He ain't nothing but a washed up junkie. Shit, he's been locked up so many times that jail is like home to him," Moreno joked.

"Moreno, you are a fool. I just hope he plays ball and keeps his mouth shut," Milton stated.

"He'll keep his mouth shut if he knows what's good for him. If not, I got people inside that can take care of that situation easily. We don't have anything to worry about at all," Moreno promised him.

"That's what I like to hear. You know we don't do messy business. Here's something extra for your troubles compliments of the big man," Milton stated referencing Geno. He tossed him a stack of hundred dollar bills that added up to ten grand. Moreno's facial expression change quickly. The money was enough to make him put Raven on the back burner for a minute.

"Thanks, cuz. You know I always got your back. Hey, why was Geno worried about that murder case anyway?" Moreno asked.

"I have no clue and don't want to know. He's a smart man. I'm sure he has his reasons," he replied.

"It's all good with me. Whenever you need something done, I'm your man," Moreno stated confidently while he fanned himself off with the stack of money.

Their conversation was interrupted when Milton's cell phone rang. When he answered it, his entire facial expression changed. He pounded his hand on the desk and began cursing out loud. It was Pauletta on the other end of the phone.

"We've gotta go, man. We've gotta go to the hospital! Jarvis has been shot! My brother has been shot!" Milton yelled with tears in his eyes. He threw his phone at the wall and it shattered in pieces.

"What the hell? This can't be real! Let's go!" Moreno stated.

They made a mad dash to exit the club. They hopped in Moreno's truck in route to the hospital. Milton's mind just raced with thoughts of revenge against whoever did this to his brother. They were twins and shared a deeper connection than most brothers. He had to survive was all Milton said to himself the entire ride to the hospital.

Chapter 24

Tragically, Jarvis succumbed to his injuries three days after he was shot. Milton and Pauletta were by his side when he took his last breath. Geno and the rest of their crime family were all there for Milton to offer their unwavering support in this most trying time. Milton was overcome with grief and inconsolable. He broke down at Jarvis' funeral and refused to let the funeral home staff close his casket. Geno had to comfort him and convince him that Jarvis was gone and there was nothing he could do to bring him back.

Pauletta was just as distraught particularly after she found out Jarvis had planned to ask her to marry him as a surprise for their upcoming anniversary. Moreno was steaming mad as well. He wanted revenge so bad he could taste it on the tip of his tongue. Jarvis and Milton were more like brothers than cousins to him. Geno had to calm him down and advise him they would have a chance to get revenge very soon, but for now they needed to lay low.

After his father's death recently, Geno took Jarvis' death especially hard. He blamed himself for Rah having the opportunity to kill him because he left him alive when he took out the rest of Nesta's crew. He made the biggest mistake a General could make when engaged in war: he let his enemy live only to rise up again and pose a problem once he regrouped. The reason he let Rah live was because he didn't see him as much of a threat. His miscalculation cost him a dear friend in Jarvis. He almost lost Sal as well had he not been on point when Rah's goons came to kill him. Geno would have to live with this mistake for the rest of his life.

The first thing Geno had to do was to find out exactly where Rah was located. He had been off the grid since his father's death. He had heard that he shut down his magazine as well as his store in Baltimore and left town for good. Geno put John Lucci on the case to find him and he delivered as usual. It took him a few days to use some of his contacts to find out that Rah had relocated to Miami. He found out that Rah had imported a slew of his family members from Jamaica to help him resume the marijuana distribution business that his cousin, Liddell, originally established in the city. His operation was on a much smaller scale than what Liddell had established, but he had plans to expand over time.

To get his revenge on Rah, Geno knew he had to be smart and calculative. After the dramatic way he went about killing Nesta and his entire crew through the use of a bomb, he didn't want to draw too much attention to himself by getting rid of Rah in a similar fashion. Also, after losing Jarvis, he didn't want to put too many more of his good men at risk trying to go to war with Rah. Thus, he hatched a scheme with Jericho whereby he would to take Rah out by himself. Geno called in his marker with Jericho like he told him he would when they first met. Jericho was true to his word and agreed to do the job. Once he got the information about Rah's whereabouts from John Lucci, he hopped on a plane to Miami to do what he did best.

Once he touched down in Miami, Jericho checked into a low rent motel under an alias. He used a map of the city to locate Rah's home. To Jericho's surprise, Rah didn't live in a grand estate like his father did. Nesta believed in doing things big like Geno, but Rah was just the opposite. He lived a very low key lifestyle. Jericho discovered that he stayed in a modest three bedroom townhome located near the beach. He noticed he didn't have a security detail around his home because everybody knew him in the small community and he felt safe around them.

Jericho observed his comings and goings for almost two weeks before he had his routine down pat. He decided that the best time to catch him vulnerable was when he went to a local Jamaican lounge called the Tea Tree. It was a small bar up the street from his home that served Caribbean food and drinks. Rah went there three times a week and would stay there for a few hours before he called it a night. On this particular night, it was close to one o'clock in the morning when Jericho saw him leave out. He decided it was time for him to make his move.

Jericho wore a mask to conceal his identity. He watched Rah as he got in his car and swooped down on him from behind. Before Rah had a chance to react, Jericho injected him in the jugular vein with a syringe filled with etorphine, which knocked him out cold. Jericho knew he would be unconscious for at least thirty minutes. That was more than enough time for him to get him to the location where he planned to kill him. Jericho pushed his lifeless body into the back seat of his Mercedes and drove off.

It took Jericho around twenty minutes before he reached his destination. He had found an abandoned building in South Florida that was perfect for what he had in mind for Rah. He dragged his body inside of the building. He tied up his hands and feet. Seated right next to him, he had a large cage that contained five hungry pit bulls that were ready to eat. He purchased them from a local Hispanic pit bull breeder who trained his dogs for just this purpose. Jericho waited patiently for Rah to wake up. When he finally did, he was groggy and confused.

"Where the hell am I? Who the hell are you?" he asked as he looked around the abandoned warehouse. Jericho just laughed at him as he attempted to squirm his way out of the ropes.

"I'm your worst nightmare. Somebody wants to talk to you," Jericho stated. He took out his phone and called Geno. When he answered, he put the phone in speaker mode.

"Rah, how is it going, buddy?" Geno asked jokingly. Rah instantly recognized his voice.

"Geno, you son of a bitch, you killed my father and you thought I would let that ride? That's why I killed your partner. The other one was lucky he got away," Rah boasted. Even though he knew he was about to die, he didn't care. He didn't have much to live for anymore now that his father was dead and their organization was destroyed. He was a defeated man.

"Just like your father, you tried to play a game you're not equipped to play. Yes, you killed Jarvis and he was like a brother to me. I should have killed you when I killed your father. That was my mistake, but I won't make it twice. Jericho let the dogs loose on his ass and send him on his way to Hell. I want to listen while they take large bites out of his ass," Geno stated sadistically.

Right on cue, Jericho threw several raw steaks near where Rah was seated. He opened up the cage to let the dogs out. They feasted on the steaks and when they were done, they proceeded to devour Rah. The vicious animals bit chunks of his flesh as he screamed out in agony. There was no one in the surrounding area to hear his cries. Jericho simply stood there and observed the attack. He recorded it all with camera on his phone for Geno to view at a later date. Once, he saw that Rah was dead, he exited the warehouse on his way to the airport to catch a plane back to Baltimore.

Chapter 25

"Are you sure you have everything you need?" Carina asked Gianna.

"Yes, I'm sure. I'm ready to go so I can hit the beach. I need to work on my tan," Gianna stated excitedly. She was at the age where her body had begun to fill out and all of the cute boys in school took notice.

"And I will be right there with you to make sure you behave yourself," Carina responded in a motherly tone.

With all of the drama and death he experienced in his life recently, Geno needed a vacation just to clear his head. He talked things over with Sal and arranged for him to run things at the Foundation in his absence. Cesare agreed to assist him as needed. There was a time when Geno didn't feel comfortable leaving his company in the hands of someone else to run, but things had changed dramatically with Cesare and Sal as his go to guys. Consequently, Geno made plans to take Carina and the children to the Bahamas for two weeks for some family fun time. It was a much needed trip because it had been almost three years since their last family vacation.

Geno was packing the last of their things in the back of the truck when he forgot that he left his new HD camera in the house. He quickly ran back inside to retrieve it out of his home office. Once he found it, he made his way back outside to prepare to leave. He had chartered a private plane that would be leaving out of Martin State Airport. He hopped in the truck and pulled off. Their flight would be leaving in two hours so they had plenty of time to get there.

As he drove down his winding driveway, he noticed something strange. There were several marked cars headed in his direction with their lights flashing. In no time, the cars had them surrounded. There were federal agents everywhere. Carina and the children were terrified. Geno did his best to calm them down.

"Geno Caprese, step out of the vehicle with your hands up!" he heard a voice state loudly.

"Relax, Carina. This has to be a mistake. I'll straighten this all out and we will be on our way," Geno stated calmly.

He opened up the driver's side door and exited the vehicle. He shook his head in disbelief. Somebody would have to pay for scaring his wife and children like this. As he stood with his arms raised, one of the agents walked toward him with a document in his hand.

"Geno Caprese, you are under arrest for income tax evasion and money laundering. You have the right to remain silent. Anything you say can and will be used against you. You have the right to an attorney......."

Geno knew the entire spill because he reminded his clients of their Miranda rights all of the time. He put his hands behind his back as the detective placed him in handcuffs. He glanced over at Carina and his children, who had now gotten out of the truck. His heart sunk in his chest. He was furious because this was a scene he never wanted his children to see with him being taken off to jail. He was escorted over to one of the unmarked cars and placed in the back seat. He couldn't wait to make his one phone call so he could get to work on figuring out who snitched on him.

To be continued

Coming soon!

High Society Gangster
III

The final chapter

Other titles available by Thomas Long:

Dayvon's Story: A Thug's Life
Just Like Daddy
Money Kings: Just Like Daddy 2
Takeisha's Song: Cash Rules Everything
Unconventional Love
The Bodymore Homicide Novella series
Love TKO
High Society Gangster

You can also find out additional information on Thomas Long at:

www.tlongwrites.com

http://www.tlongwrites.com/apps/blog

http://www.amazon.com/Thomas-Long/e/B0058OVYC6/

Facebook:

https://www.facebook.com/pages/Thomas-Long/169575816453538

Twitter and Instagram: @tlongmoney

www.ingramcontent.com/pod-product-compliance
Lightning Source LLC
Chambersburg PA
CBHW031611240626
47153CB00002B/717